Metaphorosis

February 2021

Beautifully made speculative fiction

Also from Metaphorosis

<u>Verdage</u>

Reading 5X5 x2: Duets
Score – an SFF symphony
Reading 5X5: Readers' Edition
Reading 5X5: Writers' Edition

<u>Metaphorosis Magazine</u>

Metaphorosis: Best of 20xx
Metaphorosis 20xx: The Complete Stories
annual issues, from 2016

Monthly issues

<u>Plant Based Press</u>

Best Vegan Science Fiction & Fantasy
annual issues, from 2016

<u>Vestige</u>

Tower of Mud and Straw
by Yaroslav Barsukov

<u>from B. Morris Allen</u>

Susurrus
Allenthology: Volume I
Tocsin: and other stories
Start with Stones: collected stories
Metaphorosis: a collection of stories

Metaphorosis

February 2021

edited by
B. Morris Allen

ISSN: 2573-136X (online)
ISBN: 978-1-64076-193-3 (e-book)
ISBN: 978-1-64076-194-0 (paperback)

Metaphorosis
a magazine of speculative fiction

from
Metaphorosis Publishing

Neskowin

February 2021

Vacation Gnomes....................................7
    by Aaron DaMommio

Rock-Adda's World...............................37
    by Chloe Smith

Endless...73
    by Ted S. Bushman

Reach for Your Ocean Heart.................125
    by C.M. Fields

Vacation Gnomes

Aaron DaMommio

Amy wrestled the key into the beach house door with one hand while balancing her phone on her shoulder, the whole operation complicated by the tote bag weighing down one arm. Her mom spoke in her ear. "Do you really mean Colin won't be joining us for Christmas?"

"We're on a break, Mom. If I understood it, it probably wouldn't be happening."

"Now, don't say that. He's the one who needs to come to his senses."

Amy appreciated her mom's loyalty. She just wasn't sure she deserved it. "He seemed pretty clear about the whole thing," she said. She'd never worried about Colin and commitment. The trouble with Colin was getting him to change his mind.

But she was here to stop thinking about Colin. She needed to leave that behind, or what kind of a vacation would this be? She'd decided when she planned this: the trip would be all about New Amy, who didn't obsess about guys.

She jiggled the handle and the door popped open. She managed to hop inside and kick it shut without dropping anything. She wrinkled her nose. Had the last tenants forgotten to empty the trash can? How long *had* this place been empty?

The midday sun filtering in through the slats of the blinds was enough to show that the downstairs was about what she expected: a small white kitchen opening onto a blue living room with lots of white wicker furniture and the kind of matchy-matchy design that never happened in houses people actually lived in.

She ignored the living room and headed for the kitchen. It was her first time in one of these rentals, but she'd memorized the layout; her company rented dozens just like it. This one was farther from the beach than most, which was why it had been available when her boss forced her to finally take a vacation. She'd been so annoyed at the order that she decided to mark the property as occupied for the week. After three years in property management, she knew how to hide her tracks. As long as it was pristine when she left in a week, no one would be the wiser.

She hefted the tote bag onto the kitchen island while her mom continued speaking in her ear, trying to make a connection between Amy's situation and the ups and downs of living with Amy's father.

Amy dumped out the tote bag to reveal a six-pack of wine coolers, a baggie of celery sticks, and a packet of Oreos. The balanced lunch of a mature twenty-eight-year-old.

She stared at the Oreos. Colin's idea of a serving of Oreos was half a bag, and he still didn't gain weight. It wasn't fair.

It really wasn't fair.

"No, I don't know what Colin was thinking," Amy said. "You'd have to ask the bastard yourself." Her mom started to reply. "Oh, no," Amy laughed. "Please don't actually call him. Thanks. Bye."

She set the phone down on the island with the rest of her junk. She hated lying to her mom. A break? Sure, he'd said that. But he'd also mentioned seeing other people.

Amy knew what that meant. He wanted to break up with her, he just didn't want to say it. She just wished she knew why.

It wasn't so long ago that Colin had seemed perfect. He never did that threaten-to-break-up-constantly thing like Jason back in college. Nor did he have the idealism of Paul, whose passion made her giddy ... until he disappeared to teach English in Bangladesh.

Colin had a steady job at a bank, he didn't overindulge, he was polite to waitstaff. His biggest flaw was that he didn't like to dance. What did it matter if she ended up dancing alone to videos she found on the net?

Of course, it was Colin who'd announced they needed a break. Which was in a way what created New Amy. She dated the start of New Amy from when Colin made his declaration, because that was when she had marched over to Colin's place for a two-hour shouting match that left her a wreck the next day at work.

Followed by her boss insisting she take some of those vacation days she'd piled up.

Ugh. All she wanted to do right now was veg out in front of the TV. She could catch up on the last few episodes of *Celebrity Dance Death Match.*

Her eyes travelled from the Oreos to the wine coolers. She yanked one out of the six-pack, twisted off the top, and took a swig. She glanced at the label. Berry something. It'd do, but one six-pack wouldn't last long.

Unless she restocked at Colin's parent's nearby beach house. Now, *that* was a New Amy sort of thought.

Points in favor: it was only a few blocks away. It had a vast wine cellar. Colin's parents never went there anymore. Amy knew which plastic rock they hid the spare key under.

Points against: Colin might be there. She didn't want another fight, and she definitely didn't want him to think she'd chosen this particular beach house because it was near his.

Satisfying as it might be to raid their wine cellar, it was a spectacularly bad idea.

Instead, she opened the Oreo packet and popped one in her mouth, pressing it against the roof of her mouth with her tongue until it cracked in half, while slipping the rest of the Oreos into the pocket of her lime-green hoodie. Colin's hoodie. He'd actually asked for it back while they were arguing. That was when she stopped trying to reason with him.

She shook her head. New Amy time. Obsessing over Colin was what had led to that scene where she ended up yelling at a customer on the phone. Her boss hadn't cared that the guy couldn't decide whether he wanted to vacation in Miami or Key West. Didn't matter that she'd never yelled at anyone before. To her boss, this proved she needed to take some vacation.

Well, she would prove she could vacate with the best of them. Amy picked up the six-pack so she could head for the couch, grabbed the open wine cooler with her other hand, and took a sip. She frowned. Did not pair well with Oreos.

She took a deep breath, then wrinkled her nose again. "Did somebody leave a diaper lying around?"

Remind the clients all you wanted, they'd still forget to empty the trash ... but the kitchen trashcan was empty. She opened the fridge a crack, but it was spotless, except for a styrofoam takeout container holding two egg rolls.

She heard something from the living room. She stepped to the doorway between kitchen and living room and looked towards the entertainment center. A movement caught her eye, something heading for the couch, fast.

Ugh, were there mice in this place? If it was mice, there sure were a lot of them. She swiveled her head to follow the shapes moving across the couch now, like water flowing down a rocky hill.

Except the rocks were cheap throw pillows, the hill was the couch, and the water was a cascade of four-inch-tall men with purple and orange hair, wearing only loincloths and tattoos.

Amy froze, blinked her eyes three times, and looked again. A tide of tiny dudes flowed toward her, their squeaks and warbles resolving into battle cries, echoing as they ran under the coffee table toward the kitchen. And her.

The chorus of high-pitched voices broke her shock. Amy dropped the six-pack right in front of them.

It shattered against the tile floor, icy droplets splashing her legs, glass shards tinkling. But at least it made the man-tide pause. For a second.

Then the whole mass of them shook their shaggy manes and shouted.

Amy spun around to run for the front door, but found that upwards of thirty of them had flanked her, brandishing tiny spears. One waved a sewing needle in a circle, then stabbed her foot. Amy yelped and grabbed her toe. Now there was blood on her favorite sandals.

She raised a foot angrily for a stomp, and they scattered. She ran from the kitchen to the only enclosed space within reach — the hall bathroom.

She shut the door and leaned against it, sucking in deep gulps of air. That was a mistake. It smelled like a locker room. She saw movement and stopped. There were a dozen of the little weirdos already in there with her, running in and out of a hive of toilet-paper tubes, glued together in a mound on the counter.

She still had the last wine cooler in one hand, but she snatched up a plunger with the other. "Get out, get out, *get out!*" she shouted, flailing at them with her rubber weapon. They yammered like a bunch of sopranos, but held their ground.

Amy got angry. She stopped randomly thrashing around and aimed for one, trapping it under the plunger, mashing the plunger down.

She heard a scream. She stopped mashing as the trapped fellow's pals yanked at the edges of the rubber dome. When she pulled the plunger away, there was one figure lying still underneath it. She let out her breath when he leaped up.

The little guys had had enough. Amy opened the door and they ran out. She grabbed up the cardboard hive and threw it after them with a yell. Then she slammed the door.

Amy set the wine cooler down, dropped the plunger, and turned on the hot water, keeping a finger in the stream to test the temperature. When it was hot enough, she splashed her face over and over.

Tiny men. Ridiculous. Her first alone time in forever, and she was already seeing things. She splashed some more. Then she grabbed a hand towel and dabbed at her face.

She glanced down. Little bits of brown cardboard littered the floor. The smell in the room. She wasn't hallucinating that.

She turned on the fan, looking at the wine cooler on the sink counter. She'd only drunk about a quarter of it. Even downing the whole thing wouldn't be enough to make her see things.

Still. They couldn't be real, could they? Colin liked to say she imagined things. Of course that was when she asked why he was always staying late, working weekends, or going on fishing trips. Why he was always distracted, always tired.

But Colin wasn't here. Maybe she was crazy, and maybe she wasn't, but right now she was stuck in a bathroom while a bunch of miniature Tarzan extras were out there trashing a beach house she wasn't even supposed to be using. She couldn't have imagined that. Maybe it made sense to freak out a little.

Trouble was, she didn't have the energy right now to do a proper freakout. She felt all used up. She really did need a vacation.

She wondered what Colin would do if he saw these little men. Set out traps for them, she supposed. He'd probably scoff at her for being too tenderhearted to smash one. Although if recent behavior was any indication, he'd ignore the things until they got right up in his face, then blame it all on her. But that wasn't how New Amy rolled.

She cracked the door. The little men were milling about. Some of them lay prone next to the puddle of wine cooler, singing or chanting.

Others were moving in big groups, swaying and waving their spears. Had to be a hundred of 'em. She'd faced down a dozen, but a hundred?

Still, she couldn't stay in the bathroom forever. Out of a hundred tiny men, surely one of them would see reason. She took a deep breath, readied her plunger, and opened the door.

Five of them were set up in front of the bathroom, with one fellow standing, arms crossed, on an inverted yogurt cup. Behind them were scattered groups all the way from the bathroom to the couch, where she could see trash piled up into shapes like the hive from the bathroom.

Amy squatted down for a closer look.

The little men were still making a lot of noise, but at this level she could start to make out some of the sounds. The ones by the puddle of wine cooler were repeating one chant over and over, something like "lowhall".

She turned her attention to the delegation by the yogurt cup. "What do you guys want, anyway?" Amy said.

The one on the yogurt stage said something to the four below him, who all gabbled responses until the one on top said a sharp word. The yogurt guy was tall compared to the others. He wore a half-cape on his shoulders in addition to the regulation loincloth. He held a bottle cap form one of the wine coolers in both hands like a tray; it was full. He had to squeak at Amy for a while before she realized he was repeating the same word. Lowhall? Lo-hawk-sall?

"Lohoxal?" she said. They gabbled at each other in excitement, then the yogurt guy did a sort of dance. He waved the bottle cap at her again, looking at her with eyebrows raised. He wanted more.

Amy thought about the wine cooler perched on the bathroom counter. She hadn't really planned on sharing. "Sure, I've got more," she said. "But you guys realize you can't stay here, right?"

They squeaked at each other some more then looked up at her. Amy sighed. She did a fingers-walking-across-her-hand gesture. The yogurt guy danced some more.

"Well if dancing's what you want..." She did some moves from a video she'd seen recently for a pop song about a nasty breakup, trying to convey that these dudes needed to move on down the road.

The more she danced, the more excited yogurt guy became. But he wasn't agreeing with her, she began to understand. He was trying to tell her a story.

He kept returning to a move that involved fingers to his ears while he leapt around and shook an imaginary tail. Slowly she got the picture: a pointy-eared creature — a cat? — that chased them to here, to the beach house.

She supposed it wouldn't have to be much of a cat to be a danger to these little guys. Then he started counting heads, and gesturing at the sky... she had the impression he was trying to tell her how long they'd been here, but she wasn't sure.

She did another short dance to encourage him to continue. She pointed at a group of the men, and he bobbed his head. She looked past the troops at the holes cut in the couch, with stuffing pulled out. Empty Chinese-food boxes and chip bags turned into tents. Evidence of a growing population.

They went back and forth for a while to get the numbers right, until she decided he was trying to tell her that maybe thirty of the little men had arrived here a month ago.

There was still a big group gathered by the wine cooler puddle, and it was organized. They took turns drinking from the puddle, slowly, reverently. Amy shook her head and focused her attention on Yogurt Leader Guy. "Where did you come from, anyway?"

When that confused him, she put together a short miming dance. She'd never let anyone at work know about her dancing, but now all the time she'd spent mimicking videos paid off. She had moves ready for who, what, where, and why.

The cultural divide seemed like a canyon, but with a lot of repetition, they managed to get a few things straight. Either yogurt guy or maybe his grandparents had landed on the beach in the shells of, probably, turtles, roped together into something like a great hollow raft, after leaving an island where Amy gathered they were either the subjects of an atomic experiment or got cursed by a witch doctor — they didn't share enough mutual concepts for Amy to be sure.

Soon after they had arrived here, they were attacked by what sounded like a demonic tabby. They had taken shelter in this vacant beach house, where they were delighted by all the food they found, except, apparently, the egg rolls.

"You can't stay here," Amy tried to convey, but she was pretty sure the command didn't land. The beach house was all that Yogurt Guy had ever known, and he was not, it seemed, a young man. Gnome. Whatever.

She started into a dance about how a family with children would arrive here in a week, but Yogurt Guy wasn't bothered by the idea of small people. He'd clearly never spent a summer babysitting. She tried to start over, but the leader stamped his feet on top of the yogurt cup so that it made a crackling sound. He was determined to stay.

As the leader got angrier, Amy got distracted. She was captivated by the crowd near the rapidly disappearing puddle of wine cooler. After each micro-man drank deep, he'd walk away, getting more and more unsteady, until he fell over a couple of feet away. The prone ones swelled up like balloons. Some of them split open, and from each of those ... two new guys crawled out.

"Lohoxal! Lohoxal! Lohoxal!" went the chant, while Amy tried to comprehend what she was seeing. It made her lunch want to come back up. She struggled to keep it down; it hadn't been that great the first time.

But while she wobbled, the leader continued dancing, incensed now that she wasn't paying attention. She realized he'd reached his limit when he turned and shouted something.

The groups of men behind him suddenly stopped their swaying and lined up all their spears. They began to march forward.

Amy dashed toward the kitchen to grab her phone, then whirled back toward the bathroom, but a phalanx of the little men moved to block her way. She spun toward the stairs, and they followed. She twisted back about halfway up to use the plunger to shove them back, then ran higher. They chased her through the master bedroom and out onto the balcony, where she slid the glass door shut and watched them beat themselves against it in desperation.

Amy paced the balcony, stopping occasionally to stare at the army on the other side of the glass door. It was like watching a silent movie. The men danced angrily at each other. She was sure they were planning something.

Looking over the balcony rail to the drop below it, she felt caged. In nature shows, she'd always sort of rooted for the lions, but now she felt more and more like a gazelle. She circled the patio furniture: a forlorn metal vase with a dead bamboo, a pair of shiny aluminum chairs surrounding a table. She grabbed a chair and sat down, eating an Oreo while staring at her cell phone.

She *could* call 911, but then she figured everything would come out. One photo of the downstairs would be all it would take to end her career in the vacation rental industry.

She could call her mom, but what to tell her? No way she'd believe this. Her sister would probably drive out, if only to laugh at Amy's predicament, but that would take hours.

There was one person she knew who could get here quickly. If he was at the beach house, he could be over here in minutes. Sure, they were on the outs, but this ... this was an emergency. They'd been together for more than four years; he'd understand.

She looked through the glass. There were more of the little men gathered in front of it now, and they'd found a broom.

Focus, she told herself. This call might be humiliating, but it would keep her alive. She wasn't going to let them stab her toes again. She dialed Colin.

"Amy?" he answered.

Her heart was beating fast. "Colin? Are you at the beach house?"

He paused before answering. "I mean, yes —"

"Ok, whew, good," she said. "Listen, weird question, but —"

"Amy, I thought we agreed we need time apart."

"Actually, you didn't give me a choice, Colin, but that's neither here nor —"

Then Amy heard a voice in the background. "Who's that on the phone?" A woman's voice.

Amy hung up.

Tears filled her eyes. She let them fall, penetrating the metal mesh of the patio table to drip onto her jeans.

Amy sat on the balcony for a long time.

She wanted to tell herself it couldn't be true. But she'd been in denial for too long already; she was ready to move on to anger.

Endless fishing trips. Late nights at the office. It was so obvious now, she had to laugh. She'd checked for all kinds of flaws, never seeing how the whole of Colin added up to such a bastard.

She'd let him convince her their problems were her fault.

She glanced at the little men. They were no longer milling around aimlessly. She approached the sliding door and saw that they were all gathered in two lines, perpendicular to the door. Between them was the broom handle, barely recognizable at this point. They'd fashioned handholds on it with carpet nails, and they'd painted it in bright colors. Suddenly they all threw their hands up in the air, and took hold. They lifted the stick up and started moving towards the door, slowly at first, then at a run.

"Holy crap!" Amy said. She scurried to open the door before they could hit the glass, but she was too late. It hit the door with a plink. All the tiny men fell down. Then they jumped up and started yelling silently at one another.

That was when Amy decided she'd had enough of waiting for someone to save her. New Amy wasn't the type to wait. Who knew what these disgusting little chauvinists would do next? She pulled hard on the sliding door.

"Hey! No need to get violent," she said. "I just needed some me time."

They were trying to get organized after the failure of their battering ram. Amy picked up the metal vase from the balcony and rolled it toward the little men so that they had to dodge out of the way, then she followed it in. When a group at the back rallied, she stomped the ground hard right in front of them and they fell over.

She checked the soles of her sandals to make sure she hadn't actually squashed one, then ran for the stairs. It seemed like there was one of them on just about every step, so she slid down the banister. At the bottom, a whole company of them were stationed between Amy and the door, spears ready.

"Here, boys," she called, taking an Oreo from her pocket. She tossed it to them, and they fell on it with chaotic abandon. She glanced at the packet and shrugged, tossing it off to the side. Most of the little men followed. As their order disintegrated, Amy booked it for the door and the safety of the outside.

She could hardly believe it. She'd done it. She'd gotten out, and all by herself too.

Now what?

She squatted down and unhooked the straps of her sandals. There were tiny cuts all over her feet. She pulled the sandals off and looped the straps in one hand, then stood there, leaning on her car for a minute. Her keys, her wallet — they were in her purse, inside.

Never mind. She had a phone. She'd be okay. Distance, that was what she needed.

She was just so done with little men.

She'd made a mistake with Colin. She could admit that now. Before she met him, she'd just had that breakup with

Brock, who expected her to take care of him and got so pissy when she wouldn't. So when she met Colin, her standards were off.

Also, Colin was gorgeous. He must spend some of that fishing time working out, because he had abs like forever. Maybe not so much in the face department. But he was cute, in a vulnerable kind of way, and ... no. She couldn't think like that.

What she needed was to get angry.

She wandered down the street. She didn't care about the beach house. She wasn't going to be needing any more vacations. The tribe had solved that for her: after this fiasco, she was sure she wouldn't have a job.

No boyfriend, no job. Might as well change her name, move to Chicago. Become a dancer.

Still. An hour ago she'd been thinking she couldn't make it without Colin. She didn't want to walk away now and prove it.

When she got to the end of the street, she saw a corner liquor store. There was a sign in the window indicating that you could pay with an app, and it occurred to her that she had a six-pack of wine coolers to replace.

Once inside, she looked through the cramped store's selection. At one o'clock on a Saturday, she was the only customer. A label featuring a garden gnome caught her eye. The description cited notes of lemon, oak, and, she assumed, chauvinism. A dark red with a high alcohol content.

She'd fed the little guys cookies, but only the wine coolers seemed to trigger their weird reproduction. What, she wondered, would they do for something stronger?

She paid for the bottle with a smile.

She stood in front of the crowd of little men. They brought out their leader, whose beard now reached nearly to his toes. He had to be helped by two younger guys, but he came.

It took a lot of dancing around to explain her plan, but Amy persevered. When he seemed hesitant, she pulled her prize out of its paper bag.

She'd had the clerk back at the store loosen the cork. Now she poured out a serving into a saucer. They lowered the oldster down in front of it. On hands and knees, he sampled what Amy offered.

He looked up at her, and started to grow. Amy shuddered. She'd been right: the strength of the alcohol mattered.

In seconds, the leader sprouted a giant boil on his back. At the end of a minute it burst, letting out three new pygmies. The leader grinned, apparently unhurt. "Lohoxal," he said.

Amy shook her head. "You want more?" she said.

"Lohoxal?" he repeated. In response, Amy started to spin and twirl as she danced up a story of a trip to a nearby house where unlimited Lohoxal waited.

The plan, Amy figured, was simple. She'd pack the guys into her hatchback, let them into Colin's place, and trade alcohol for amok time, letting Colin both pay the cost and reap the dubious reward. She liked the thought of the destruction he'd find.

They arrived in late afternoon, just in time to see Colin's Mazda leaving. Amy grabbed the key from its rock, prepared to aim the guys at the cellar and depart.

But she had to help them find the cellar door, and then they were afraid to go down the stairs alone. Once down there, she saw a bottle of Beaujolais from the same batch she'd enjoyed the first time Colin brought her here.

Now, watching the little men team up to drag bottles out of racks, she decided that the Beaujolais had been the best thing about that weekend. She'd spent half of it by herself while Colin fished; the rest, they'd spent arguing.

She drank to the memory until she heard a crash. The boys had misjudged the weight of a bottle and it'd cracked on the slab floor, spraying red in a yard's radius. Amy was ready to tell them not to worry about it—she'd expected her revenge to get a little messy—but then there was the thump of footsteps overhead. The sound startled a second group into dropping their bottle, making another ruddy puddle.

Dozens of tiny eyes looked at Amy. "Oh boy," she said. She made a shooing motion, fingers spread wide. One gnome nodded and started barking orders as the others gathered into small groups. Amy couldn't watch; she had to run to the foot of the stairs to flip off the light switch and then hide behind a wine rack.

She froze while the sounds of little bodies moving seemed impossibly loud in the darkness. A beam of light appeared when the door at the top of stairs opened. She heard Colin say, "I'll get some paper towels," then the click as he flipped the sibling switch and turned the light back on.

Amy covered her eyes. Colin would have to see the broken bottles, then he'd look further, and then he'd find her down here.

Colin came all the way down the stairs. Amy peeked through her fingers as he pawed at a shelf, swore at something, and then started back up the stairs.

She looked at the space in front of the wine racks. The blood-red puddle was gone. Only a single dark shard of glass lingered in the center of the pale concrete floor. Somehow, the guys had erased their trail.

Then she heard Colin's voice again as he reached the top. "I'm going to have to get some traps," he said to someone upstairs. "There's mouse crap all over the place down there."

Amy looked around for the bottle of Beaujolais, then snapped her fingers when she remembered it was on the other side of the room. There hadn't been much left, anyway, judging from the tears that filled her eyes when she pictured a tiny orange-haired figure squirming in a mousetrap.

There was really only one thing to do after that.

Back at the rental, Amy stood in the kitchen and dialed for Chinese while the guys built scaffolds to organize the wine so as to keep the corks wet, a practice they took very seriously once she explained it. She was sure one of them had a clipboard.

Her exit from a cellar window hadn't been dignified, and she'd never be able to wear those pants again, but without the pushing and pulling of twenty of the little fellows, she'd never have made it out. Not to mention the wine bottles they'd hoisted out using a water hose.

Forty or fifty more were in the living room now, divided into squads of five as they tackled cleanup. They sang as they worked; thankfully, they didn't incline to whistling.

"Twenty-four orders of lemon chicken. Yes, twenty-four. I understand, I can wait." She glanced at the living room. The work crews were forming up into a line; apparently, it was time for a dance break. "Oh, and no egg rolls."

Now that she felt like she wasn't going to lose her job, she'd started to think about the possibilities that a team of whip-fast workers presented. She happened to know a company that could use a crack Make Ready crew, able to handle any job, no matter how big ... or small.

But there was no hurry. She still had the place for four days; plenty of time to figure something out. In the meantime, the guys were waving at her.

She joined them in the living room. It felt nice not to dance alone.

See Aaron DaMommio's story "Vacation Gnomes" online at Metaphorosis.
If you liked it, leave a comment. Authors love that!
Remember to subscribe to our e-mail updates so you'll know when new stories are posted.

About the story

"Vacation Gnomes" was originally developed in 2017 for the Codex online writing group's Weekend Warrior competition, where you have to put together a 750-word story in a weekend. I love how this process crystallizes an Idea down to its essentials. Since you want to get something that has the shape and satisfying ending of a whole story in such a tiny package, you really have to keep pushing to get your character through some kind of arc, and you have to throw almost everything overboard to meet the wordcount limit.

My notes say that it was based on a prompt about 'filthy dwarves', but I barely remember that now. I developed an image of a woman finding that her vacation place was infested with tiny, messy gnomes. By the end of the contest weekend I had the basic plot found here, of a woman distracted by a breakup who has to find a way to deal with a lot of very small men, all by herself.

A question for the author

Q: Do you use music for inspiration? If so, what do you listen to?

A: I don't typically use music for inspiration directly. I've certainly tried having a playlist for a specific project, with the idea of getting back into the right frame of mine for that project, but I dropped that after I created a ton of playlists in a service that didn't survive the first big internet company implosion, and I haven't gone back to the practice since then.

On the other hand, I love song lyrics, especially ones that involve wordplay. In general, I usually take inspiration from wordplay and permutations. I love to see where a prompt will take me, and I enjoy it just as much when the final result is so far from the original prompt no other eyes can see the path.

About the author

Aaron DaMommio is a husband, father, writer, and juggler who came to Austin, Texas, for college and never left. During the day he tries to make the world safe for a team of technical writers who need support navigating the strange hierarchies of XML. He has three children and a share in four dogs. On a good day he can name all the dwarves from *The Hobbit*.

aarondamommio.blogspot.com

Rock-Adda's World

Chloe Smith

Adda felt that the greatest mystery of being a parent was the way it tied you, with such powerful bonds of love, to a person with whom you would continuously fail to communicate successfully.

She always looked forward to her daughter's yearly visits, even though they always meant more arguments that left her feeling both guilty and misunderstood. Cia usually waited until the last possibility of storm was long gone and the warm season was fully established, but this year icy rime crunched under Adda's boots as she walked out to greet her daughter, and cold air pressed against the exposed skin of her face and hands.

Cia turned from pulling a bag out of her suborbital hopper. She was certainly dressed for the cold, in thermal layers whose slim profile spoke volumes about their cost. Adda felt the usual mixture of wonder and pride that this person, who had once lain asleep with her head below Adda's chin and her feet on her stomach, was now flying herself between continents in a rented jet.

Cia said, "Why aren't you wearing gloves, Ma?"

Adda laughed. "Which one of us is the mother here, girl?"

Cia wiggled well-covered fingers. "*I'm* dressed appropriately. I was brought up well."

Adda scoffed and gave her a squeeze around the shoulders. "Well, come on in, then. I knew we were barely going to be out."

Her observation station was a small building, half-sunk in the ground, with its own power panels and the bulk of a skimplane hangar visible off to one side. Adda gave the hangar walls a furtive once-over as she held the door of the main building open for Cia—yes, there was nothing more than a shadowy smudge, indistinguishable from weathering. No one now would be able to tell that yesterday she had woken to find a block-lettered scrawl: STAND BACK AND SHUT UP, ROCK-LOVER.

It had taken her most of a morning, and a lot of retching, to clean out the mess of garbage and refuse they had left on and around her skimplane, and another couple of hours to repair and reinforce the damaged locks. Adda had forced down the feelings of outrage and violation, telling herself that fear was capitulation. This was an expression of popular opinion, not a direct threat—there was no sabotage to the vehicle itself, and no attack on her actual living space.

Yet, Cia would say if she knew. Adda didn't plan on telling her.

Inside, Cia settled herself in the second sleeping quarters. They were officially designated for visiting researchers, but Adda had been thinking of them as "Cia's," reserved for her semi-annual visits, for at least the last five years.

Adda made tea in the closet-like canteen, and then brought it out to her dining-cum-work table, where she had to push the clutter of battery packs and recording equipment farther back to make room for two.

"How are things?" she asked when Cia reappeared, preparing herself for at least a half hour of free-form rambling on Cia's work- and love-life, helped along by Adda's occasional interested noise or leading question.

Cia shrugged. "They're good. Same-same but different. How are *you* doing, though?"

Uh oh. It looked like they weren't going to pretend that things were casual for even as long as Adda had hoped. "What makes you ask?" She gave her daughter a look.

Cia had the grace to look uncomfortable. "Well," she said, "you know we end up being party to a lot of the discussion around new settlement development..." Cia worked for the city manager's office in Istvan, the oldest city on the South Continent. Her position often gave her a line on issues that impacted the cetalith population, though not from a perspective that Adda could agree with. She gritted her teeth in anticipation as Cia continued, "there's been—well, I saw the footage of the town hall meeting. I was worried about you."

Adda closed her eyes. *I was worried about you.* Not, *How could they?* Not, *The situation's appalling.* Not, *What can we do?*

She opened them again, stared past Cia to the wall over her terminal station, where she had pinned an excerpt from a flimsy printout:

"The giant cetaliths of Krishnan IV are another puzzling example. These silicate creatures, who move at speeds not exceeding 6 centimeters per U-hour, and leave as the marks of their passage enduring tunnels that permeate the surface of their world, may have a level of sentience that would guarantee their planet Protectorate, if not Sovereign, status under the Cygni Accords. Although they are solitary beings, whose paths cross only occasionally over the course of their long, long lives, their 'songs,' which gave rise to the name 'whales of stone,' may be a form of communication. This implies a level of sophistication and consciousness, but researchers have yet to establish firm proof of either. This ambiguity has led to the current impasse in official decision-making."

The whole document, the *Report on Resources of Non-Sovereign Satellites,*

Planets, and Exoplanets, Appendix A: Sentient Fauna, was one of the supports that the first settlers had used to make their case for access to the planet. *Give us this world to do what we like with as long as we don't understand it.* Adda kept the flimsy on display as a reminder of what was at stake.

Cia was frowning at her. "Ma?"

"It's a worrying situation," she said dryly.

Cia rotated her cup in her hands. Still staring at it, she said "The thing is, speaking like that at the meeting... I don't think it does any good."

"You mean you were embarrassed." Adda's response came out harsher than she meant it to. The truth was, she had embarrassed herself. In the moment, she had been caught up in trying to convince the town shareholders to see what she saw, until she was half-shouting:

"How can we be so selfish! This isn't our world. To just come in and take what we like because it suits us—we have no right! This is an ancient species, a mystery worth unravelling! What you're doing isn't even legal—sentient-status ruling is still pending!"

Chair Horace Grish nodded impatiently, while the crowd behind Adda shifted and muttered. "That status ruling has been pending since Krishnan's was first surveyed, Doctor Oram. It's hard to believe that a decision is forthcoming. In the absence of official status—"

"You're just going to batter this planet and destroy a potentially sovereign species! The ruling isn't the point—this is wrong!"

She had felt so large at the time, full of righteousness and fire, containing multitudes. On the recording, though, her voice was thinner and higher, and she looked like what she was, an old woman, speaking words that meant nothing to her listeners.

"Ma!" Cia's voice cut through her reverie. Adda looked at her. Cia had pushed the tea aside, her forehead creased. "Who do you think is going to stop them? Continental governance? Sharevote results show there's only a minority favoring holding off expansion until the non-Sovereign ruling is official."

"I know that," Adda snapped. She had correspondents besides Cia, other scientists and citizen enthusiasts who followed her research from the southern continent, where human settlements had spread. Some shared their own work with her, their explorations of the cetalith routes that ran through this world—although that work could only be the archeology of dead spaces and still remnants. There were no moving cetaliths left on South Continent, and Adda was the only researcher who had committed to an isolated life on the northern landmass—isolated, at least, until the arrival of the recent wave of separatists from the south, who had founded the town of New Beginnings.

Cia shook her head. "How many reports have you sent, Ma? For how long? After all this time, it's not just sharevotes; most *people* don't think Cygni is going to designate the Rocks as sentient."

Adda sighed. "That's not an accurate term."

"That's not the point—"

"It *is* the point!" Adda's voice rose. "We don't understand, and our ignorance is killing them!"

"Ma!" Cia wailed, "Killing them? They're not even aware! But this could get *you* killed! New Beginnings has their own sovereignty up here. What if they decide you're disrupting the peace, or impeding growth?" She gulped, sending a pang through Adda—*You make your daughter cry.*

Cia took a deep breath, regaining control. "I know how much you care about your research, but it's been years of nothing to show. There's work you could do on the Southern Continent. Research positions in the capital, where it's safe. You're in danger here—don't try to deny it!"

Adda started to argue back, sputtering in her effort to find the words that could communicate her urgency, but Cia banged her tea down, cutting her off. She reached out to uncurl Adda's fingers from her own mug. "I love you and I'm afraid for you. Please come home with me, Ma. This isn't worth it."

There was a long pause before Adda said stiffly, "They have no right to do anything. New Beginnings didn't even have the right to incorporate, officially."

Cia dropped Adda's hands and put her head down on the table. "That doesn't seem to bother them." Even muffled, her words rang with fear and frustration.

Adda had no answer to that. Cia was right, but she didn't see the real problem.

If I can't make my own daughter understand...

She pushed herself to her feet. "You need to see for yourself. Come on."

"What? No, Ma..." Cia's protests disappeared as Adda went into her sleeping quarters to find better clothes. She was damned if she was going to let Cia mother her about gloves again.

It took 10 minutes for them to reemerge into the afternoon's chill. Cia had taken one look at her mother's outerwear, sighed deeply, and redressed herself for the elements. She followed Adda with an expression of long-suffering filial piety. *Fine.* Adda would take filial piety when she couldn't get authentic understanding.

Outside, the land was sere and rolling, irregular brown with patches of frost and the simple fungusoid varietals that were this planet's only plant parallels at this latitude. The sky above was big and deep, with thin skeins of clouds wisping across it.

Cia grimaced after they climbed into the little skimplane. "It smells like a bad batch of fertilizer."

Adda shrugged dismissively. "It's just old. Let me concentrate." The skimplane was putting her through seconds of flickering controls. Her stomach clenched. It was possible she'd missed something when she checked for sabotage this morning. She closed her eyes and mentally ran through everything she'd checked: seals, power-cells, flight mechanism, stabilizers—

The hum of the engine drive coming online interrupted her frantic listing, bringing her back to the present. Adda sighed in relief and Cia in impatience.

The horizon expanded below them as they climbed in silence, until Cia couldn't keep her peace anymore. "Ma, if you wanted to fly, we could have taken the sat'."

"Just look," Adda said, slowing the skimplane to a near-hover. Cia glanced down obediently.

At this height, the patterns on the land were easy to notice. There were the hills and gullies made by eons of landmasses pushing against each other, and the irregularities shaped by wind and this planet's scant waters moving the dust and crumbles of stone and biomass, but within the chaos-formed shapes were others—regular lines that cut across the surface of the world in mismatched arcs and segments, appearing and disappearing like poorly erased cursive.

"Think of the years they've been here," Adda said. "Think of the ages. And we came in three generations ago, spreading and spreading as humans always do. Now half of them have gone still and dead."

Cia started to say something, swallowed down her words with an effort, and put her hand over Adda's on the flight controls. Adda bit back frustration. She didn't want Cia's sympathy for her sentimental mother. She guided the skimplane back down, towards her recording site.

Adda ghosted the little craft down with the utmost possible care, so that they barely felt the settling contact with the earth. Rationally, she was aware that the evidence of harm to the cetaliths came from intense and prolonged impacts—the vibrations caused by large-scale construction, the drilling and digging that came with building energy-efficient sunken habitats and mining for the resources to support them. Irrationally, though, she didn't like the idea of adding insult to injury.

Adda tried to unobtrusively scan signs of disturbance as they disembarked. Her site closest to town had been torn apart last week, perhaps by the same enthusiast who had left their mark on her hangar. It was a relief to see that no one had come out this far. She turned back to find Cia, who was raising an eyebrow at her.

"Looking for something?"

Adda forced a grin. "Don't give me that sass. I haven't shown you anything yet." She clambered up the nearest curving slope. It was regular as the exterior of a tube, a convex arc that ran away from them for a handful of meters before disappearing into the earth. Adda dusted away the thin loose dirt with her hands (the fungusoids were not dense enough to contribute much richness or permanence to the soil), shifted a plastofiber shield that she had laid to keep out the elements, and let herself down through the hole she had painstakingly tapped in the stone.

Going by feel, she found her work lamp. Once lit, it revealed a tube-like tunnel that disappeared into darkness in both directions. Its diameter was perhaps three meters; Adda stood on a platform that she had constructed to avoid the drop to the curving floor. There was a low hum in the air, a faint rumble just on the edge of perception.

She helped Cia climb down and they set off, Adda carrying her lamp and Cia trundling dubiously in her wake. The tube curved to the right and slightly down, so the light from the opening disappeared before they had gone 100 meters. The interior surfaces were smooth enough that Adda could have walked in darkness without stumbling, but she kept the light trained on the ground in front of them, for Cia's sake. The humming continued, so low that it felt more like a pressure on the ears than a sound.

After a while, Cia said, "You've shown me pictures, Ma. And recordings."

"Witnessing is different," Adda said, and kept walking.

They reached the cetalith — #32 in Adda's research notes — after about 500 meters. Actually, it was 512 meters from her tunnel entrance, and 8 meters from where Adda had left it a week ago, going by her last marks on the tube walls. #32 was really booking it. Adda held the lamp up in silence, letting Cia take it in.

The cetalith was an immense bulk reaching up over their heads, perfectly filling the diameter of the tunnel it had made. Its irregular surface, rocky and hard as the planet itself, trembled slightly, but that was all. Its forward progression was not visible, and its moving parts, cilia that tore away the earth it swam through, were microscopic and buried in the recesses between it and the surface of the stone. Adda's earliest research had focused on those tiny, piston-like appendages, which ate away at the stone and earth of the cetalith's environment, allowed the rubble they produced to be ingested through the feeding cracks in the cetalith's forward-moving side, created the long tube it left behind, and caused the rumbling vibration that marked its passage.

It was impossible to tell the age of a living cetalith. Their digestive processes meant that they took on the mineral profiles of their surroundings at the same time that the silicate structures of their outer surfaces sloughed off with their movement, adding to the stony composition of the paths they delved. Those paths could be found running through layers of rock and sediment hundreds of thousands of years old, though. Adda had followed this particular tunnel back to where it was warped out of existence by the movements of the earth. She had seen cetalith tunnels that crossed each other, tunnels that ran together for a time, and sometimes points where two tunnels crossed and a third, new cetalith trail emerged. No one had ever witnessed behemoths meeting, though.

I need more time. These creatures don't operate on human scale. How can we give up on understanding them after a handful of years?

Next to her, Cia stood wide-eyed. Adda had a sudden memory of leading a tiny Cia out of a shuttleport gate for her first vision of the overwhelming reality of a planetside sky, the day they had arrived on Krishnan IV. Her daughter's face now had an echo of that child's wonder.

Slowly, Cia reached out a finger, before looking back at Adda questioningly. Adda nodded. "Go ahead. That's not the sort of interference that disturbs them." She watched as Cia touched the surface of the cetalith and then jerked away. Adda knew what she felt: the source of that bone-humming alien song.

"Here," Adda pulled out her handheld, and called up the audio version of her most recently collected recording. It kept the periodic, rhythmic patterns and relative intensities of the cetalith's oscillation through the earth, while translating it to a frequency within human hearing range. The noise bassooned into the tunnel, echoing away from them in the dark.

It had an irregular variation: Adda had yet to map any pattern or repeating signature in its complexity. She still had a limited data set, even though reports of cetalith song dated back to the first settlers.

The earliest builders on South Continent had spoken of feeling vibration akin to drumbeats resonating out of the stones they cut into. Adda bitterly regretted those settlers' complete lack of investigative spirit. It had been far too long before anyone had thought to make recordings, and those were compromised by human interference. Adda had spent these long years designing programs, comparing snatches and segments, consulting with seismologists and linguists, and trying to build a persuasive theory out of the conviction that this rumbling was meaningful and its source aware.

The sound washed over them for long moments, alien and opaque.

"You really believe these things deserve the world?" Cia asked. Skeptical or not, her voice was hushed.

"It doesn't matter what I believe," Adda said. "We haven't established their sentience one way or the other. There's a possibility, a space of uncertainty. If we destroy first, there's no way to ask questions later."

"Here," she took Cia's hand and laid it flat against the surface of the tunnel. After another long moment, she asked, "Do you feel that? Do you understand it? What happens if we ignore—"

"Ma, be quiet!" Cia was frowning with a sudden intensity and focus that made Adda swallow her affront and wait silently while Cia pressed both hands against the tunnel wall. The cetalith's sound was much more powerful in the earth it moved through; the vibration that transferred to a faint hum in the air around them was a call through the earth that spread outward for miles.

"Is that recording from this one?" Cia asked finally.

Adda blinked. "No. It's from 27. That's my recording point nearest New Beginnings, actually...."

Cia waved a hand furiously to silence her, the other still plastered to the wall. "Ma, it feels different now."

Adda put her hand on the wall next to Cia's, feeling the irregular hum, powerful enough this close to its source to travel up her arm. "Listen," Cia breathed, and Adda did.

The two vibrations, the recording of the cetalith amplified in the air around thcm and the living cetalith in the earth they touched, intertwined.

They stared at each other, eyes gleaming in the low light. Adda was suddenly afraid that, after this long, after so much wanting, she was tricking herself into imagining patterns where none existed. She opened her mouth, but Cia spoke first.

"I think there's some kind of rhythm or beat...?"

Adda pushed herself away from the wall, and set off back along the tunnel, almost running.

"Ma, wait!" Cia was nearly left in the dark.

Adda was short of breath by the time she reached her platform and her limbs were trembling. She bundled up half of the recording equipment she'd staged there. Thank goodness for secondary systems. By the time Cia followed her up out of the tunnel, Adda was already climbing into the skimplane.

"Is it like breathing?" Cia asked as they surged across the landscape, "Was that the first time you heard that?"

"They don't breathe. But the noise—all these years, I was only listening to one voice. You showed me—it sounds different when there are two of them. I need more data…" Adda's gaze flickered between the land ahead of them and the map display, which had the locations of all her recording points highlighted, along with an overlay of the cetalith tunnels she had mapped, topographically coded for depth.

She brought the skimplane down again on a stretch of ground free of distinguishing landmarks—but roughly halfway between the line of 32's path and another, almost parallel tunnel to the west, 33. Adda took a breath before clambering out. "Just bear with me on this—okay?"

"O-kay," Cia drew the word out, managing to telegraph skepticism and forbearance at the same time. "Can I help?"

Adda reached into the storage bench behind them for a hand-shovel. "I'm so glad you asked."

It took almost an hour for them to dig down to earth that was hard packed enough for Adda's satisfaction. "If we used an earth-mover," Cia said at one point, pulling off her hat and using it to mop her forehead, "we could be down to bedrock in half this time."

"And rain the acoustic equivalent of hellfire down on all local cetaliths in the process," Adda returned. "I'm not doing that." She continued shifting the dirt Cia was turning up, away from the hole they were creating.

Arid Krishnan IV did not have much topsoil, particularly on this continent, which lacked the forest-style growths of the south, and the earth a few feet down was so hard as to be almost indistinguishable from rock. Adda had brought all of her extra battery packs from the skimplane, as well as the recorder she had removed from the tunnel, and, most precious of all, her calibrator and "Excess Ear," the most sensitive instrument she possessed, which she usually carried with her from site to site. It took some creative fiddling to embed the Excess Ear in the dirt, connected to the secondary recorder and even more supplementary batteries. She packed loose dirt around the whole for insulation, leaving only the batteries' light receptors uncovered. She considered spraying the mound with an instant concrete for further protection, but chipping it away might upset the integrity of her recording, and it wouldn't take more than a few days to generate enough material to show—well, whatever it showed. Standing over it, she dusted off her hands. "I'm ready for dinner. Are you?"

"Ma," Cia groaned. "What's all this about?"

"I'll know when we've gotten some more information." Adda gave her daughter a hug around the shoulders. "Thanks to your help, love."

Adda spent the next three days trying not to speculate ahead of her data and failing to attend to Cia's conversations. Cia took her mother's abstraction with remarkable patience, cooked meals while Adda combed through her old recordings or stared off into space, mulling over the possibilities. She spent hours in a vain search for other segments that might resonate together, either played unmodified, or shifted upfrequency, like the tape she'd played for Cia in front of 32. She would have slept in the chair in front of her terminal, if Cia hadn't pushed her into bed each night.

"Now you know—what I went through—when you were a teen," Adda told her between yawns.

"You don't get to hold that over me anymore," Cia told her tartly, "Go to sleep, or you won't be able to make sense of your new data when you *do* get enough of it."

In fact, on the fourth morning, when Adda actually let herself start going over the overlapping recording of 32 and 33—probably too soon for a really robust dataset, but she couldn't wait anymore, and, besides, there was another town hall meeting in New Beginnings at the end of the week—it was excitement rather than exhaustion that made her hands flutter over the interface. She forced herself to take deep, steadying breaths, laying out the parameters of her analysis.

The shape of what the new recordings suggested, though, was something so massive, so revelatory, that she forgot emotions, consequences, forgot even the demands of her own body, as she started to explore her results.

Some unmeasured time later, Cia leaned over her shoulder. "Well?"

Adda input a few more commands, and then sat back as a new graphic flowed across her display. "Look."

Independently, the frequencies that sped out from each cetalith through the rigid ground appeared random, without signature or repetition. In the interference between the two frequencies, though, there was something. Caught on her analytics program, it showed resonances in recognizable periods—begun in one voice and finished in another.

Adda swallowed, half afraid to put it into words. "They're responding to each other. It's communication." She tapped at the display again, entering in another set of parameters, programs that would run back through her library of recordings, correlating timestamps, searching for echoes, trying to find patterns between what she was sure now was a symphony of voices, chorusing together underground, perceptible to those beings whose rocky bulk was attuned to the faintest shiver of frequency.

That done, she pulled up another document, and began hammering out an initial report to the research group on South Continent. Cia put a hand on her arm.

"Ma—wait. Why don't you go talk to them? Come home with me for a while; take some time to discuss what this could mean with other researchers before you write anything."

Adda frowned at her. "How can I leave now? I need to follow up on what I—what *you* found. Awareness. They recognize each other. They're talking."

Cia hesitated. "Ma... I see the pattern, but communication? What's it about? Is it a mating call? Challenge? Are they sharing the latest tips and trends?"

"Of course I don't know yet—" Adda began, irritated, but Cia cut her off.

"Exactly. You just found this and, yes, it's huge, but *we don't know yet* what it means. This isn't enough, alone, to get a

Sentience ruling from Cygni. If you come back with me, you can work on a paper about it, somewhere safe…"

"The cetaliths don't have time for me to do that!" Adda thought of the building projects going up in New Beginnings, the percussion of digging projects and construction spreading toxic shockwaves through the region's earth. She pulled her arm out of Cia's grasp and turned back to writing.

There was a long pause, during which Adda tried to think only about how best to describe her data.

Cia finally said quietly, "I know I can't stop you." Adda could feel her daughter's expression. "I just don't trust these settlers. They're dug in here, and they aren't going to listen to any new arguments about why they should wait for the ruling. Please come with me."

Shut up, Rock-Lover. Cia wasn't wrong. The memory of the sabotage and graffiti warnings hung in Adda's mind, its weight on her almost physical. If their positions were reversed, and her daughter revealed that she had been ignoring threats to her safety—well, Adda could only imagine her own fear and anger. She took a breath, but didn't look away from her display. "I can't not fight for this, love."

Cia's work-leave was up the following day, and she went back alone, resigned but clearly unhappy. She wrapped her arms around her mother before she left, and buried her faced in Adda's shoulder. "Call me every day."

Adda hugged her back and agreed, half her mind squirming with guilt, but the other half composing a new message to the Administration of Sentience Establishing Research Enterprises. There was a several-week communication lag between Krishnan IV and the nearest jump-point, a gap that had been a boon when the messages from ASERE had become more and more discouraging and she had counted on the distance to protect her from a preemptory declaration that the cetaliths weren't sovereign and the planet was free for further development. Now, though—if only she could show up in New Beginnings tomorrow with the authority of an official designation of Sentience behind her—or at least able to make the argument that this new discovery had opened some eyes at ASERE.

Cia finally released her, seemed about to say something else, but then shook her head and left with many backward glances. It was all Adda had asked for—understanding, forbearance, recognition. It was more than she deserved.

Adda arrived at New Beginnings at dusk. The sky was still luminous, although the sun had slipped below the horizon and the buildings of New Beginning were shadowed geometric mounds whose silhouettes hunched together. The door to the community meeting hall was open, and several figures were standing in its light, talking. They watched as Adda left her skimplane parked and approached, rubbing her hands together. She had forgotten her gloves again.

Adda recognized all of them; she knew almost everyone in town, at least by sight, after years of visits to what had once been an explorers' outpost and supply depot, and, more recently, months of visits to planning and development meetings after the town was established. They knew her, too.

She nodded at the group, but they didn't nod back, and as she came up to the door, a man who had been leaning against its frame shifted his bulk to stand in her way.

"Rock-Adda Oram," he greeted her, unsmiling. "Have you come to tell us our business again?"

"Sean Rios," Adda returned. "It's an open meeting, I believe."

Rios' frown deepened. The woman beside him spoke up next. "You're not a shareholder." She paused before adding, "Doctor," in a tone that made it almost a question.

Adda squared her shoulders. "I'm an expert witness. I have information—new information—that throws the status of our settlement here even further into question. This isn't our place, or our land. Under Cygni—"

"Oh, Cygni!" scoffed another man, cutting her off. "Not all this again. Didn't you get it all out of your system last time? That ruling's never gonna come—and if it does, what of it?" The group was arrayed against her now, between her and the light. "Why should we pack up and move back to South Continent, or, even worse, leave this planet that's been our home for generations, because of a bunch of *rocks*?"

Adda shoved her cold fingers into her pockets. "I just want to be heard." She took another step forward. The group of settlers drew together, the mass of their bodies cutting off the light from the doorway.

"Don't do it, Rock-Adda," Rios's voice was quiet, "Don't make it hard on yourself." He took a step forward to meet her, arms loose, while the rest looked on.

Adda stiffened her shoulders and glared at them all. She tried to imagine the words that would reach them, that would make them understand. Cygni's authority was lightyears away. Here and now, she might as well be voiceless: in the settlers' eyes, she was as devoid of meaning as the cetaliths. *Cia was right, and she'll never forgive me.*

Cia will listen to me. It wasn't the protection of policy or government, but it was what she had, what she could do.

She let her posture fall, took a step back in the face of their threat. Even shadowed by the light behind him, she could see Rios's smile, and it felt like a slap. "That's right, Doctor. That's a good choice."

She felt their eyes on her back as she walked away.

At home, she double locked the doors, and then used her terminal to call her daughter. Half a day away and to the south, Cia answered groggily, but within seconds. "Ma? Everything okay?"

Adda took another breath, steeled herself to let go. "I can't convince them, and they won't listen to me. They're making threats. No, wait—I know, you were right, but please, listen to me now. I need your help. I need the settlers to know I'm not alone up here; I need people on SoCo to know about what I've found, to believe it, to care. I know it's a lot; I know you have your own life, but this is bigger than some research project of your mother's. You saw the pattern; you felt them speak. Will you help me keep them all from falling silent?"

Cia's face on the video shifted with a mixture of emotions. Adda hoped that her words had struck a frequency her daughter could understand, that she could make her hear what the settlers were deaf to. Time that would have meant nothing on a cetalith's scale dragged by as Adda waited for her daughter's response.

Finally, Cia nodded. "Alright...." Her eyes shifted to focus on something beyond Adda's face, and her fingers came alive, tapping and shifting through her displays. "You stay where you are. I'll come get you."

Adda's heart broke a little more. "But didn't you hear what I said?"

Cia actually stopped what she was doing to roll her eyes. "I *said* alright! You want people to care about the cetaliths; you want them to understand the consequences? I'll help you tell that story, make sure it gets publicity, gets sympathy, get people to believe, maybe even commit to stopping more settlements. But that'll take time—and I'm not going to let you sit up there, vulnerable to those people. You can't make any new discoveries if you're dead. You have to leave this battlefield if you want to win the war."

Adda started to respond, but Cia didn't let her. "No! You wanted me to hear you; now hear me. I'm coming now, as soon as

I get these messages off." She cut the connection.

Adda sat in the stillness that followed, letting Cia's last words echo in her head. Finally, she turned back to her terminal, opened up her analytics program. There were still hours until Cia, even traveling at top speeds, could reach her. She pulled up the newest recording, the "conversation" between 32 and 33, and tuned it to human-audible frequencies. The alien sound filled the air around her, and Adda set herself to listening carefully, alert for signatures and repetitions in the schematic on her screen. She knew this song might be an elegy. She might not be able to stop the settlement in time, and these might be the last recorded communications of two sentient beings— but Cia was right. The fight wasn't over. There were still cetaliths who might send their resonant calls through this planet's earth for eons to come.

See Chloe Smith's story "Rock Adda's World"
online at Metaphorosis.
If you liked it, leave a comment. Authors love
that!

Remember to subscribe to our e-mail updates so you'll know when new stories are posted.

About the story

The title of this story is a terrible pun on Ursula Le Guin's first novel, *Rocannon's World*. The final product doesn't share a lot with that piece of early SF, but I began by wanting to evoke some of the same sense of a lone explorer overawed by an alien landscape. As far as where the cetaliths came from, I'm always suspicious of SF that imagines alien life that is too similar to our own. I think that if we do ever discover sentient beings on other planets, it will be so different that we'll have a hard time recognizing it as "people"—especially given that humans have a poor track record of even accomplishing so much when it comes to other groups of humans. I hope that the cetaliths are sufficiently strange and different to come across as truly alien. The bond between Adda and her daughter Cia emerged as central to the story only as I started working through my drafts. I needed someone for Adda to interact with, and once her daughter came to visit, their relationship emerged naturally as they talked together. Then I realized that Adda's own difficulties communicating—with Cia, and with other people who don't believe the cetaliths are worth understanding—could connect with her scientific discoveries and help the story say something about communication in general. That description sounds like the story evolved in a straightforward way, which is hardly the case. It went through a ton of drafts, and I'm very grateful to the friends and beta readers, and to the Metaphorosis editorial process, which helped me carve "Rock-Adda's World" into the right shape.

A question for the author

Q: What is your favorite short story?

A: This is a tough question! There is so much good short fiction out there, and I am not as well-read as I'd like to be—I feel like to select one story would be to elide many that I've loved and countless more that I haven't had a chance to discover yet. If you forced me, I'd say that one story I love for its lyricism and repurposing of traditional myths is Catherynne Valente's "Urchins, While Swimming" (*Clarkesworld*, 2006), and one whose emotional impact will never let me go is Margo Lanagan's "Singing My Sister Down" (*Black Juice*, 2004).

About the author

Chloe Smith was born and raised in the San Francisco Bay Area. Her first job ever was as a shop assistant at a SF/F-themed bookstore, and she never lost the taste for speculative fiction, although the world took her through a wide range of places and vocations before she stumbled back to her writerly ambitions. She currently works as a 7th-grade English teacher, moonlights as the proofreader for *Locus* and *Fantasy* magazines, and ekes out time in between her jobs to think up more stories about strange worlds and familiar problems.

@chloehsmith

Endless

Ted S. Bushman

In Malanihayata, the Ever-Changing City, there existed myriad ways for a smith to die.

He could leap from the eleven thousand parapets that overlooked the plains below. He could drink the poisoned air of the visitants' district, or give his mind to the flesh-recyclers. He could self-immolate within the flames of his own great forge.

There was in the Artisan's Quarter a smith called Brevin the Binder, a shaper of smartmetal, chalksteel, and soulstone; though he was friend to few in the town, his name was known in many distant cities. And he sought for a certain kind of death.

Brevin the Binder dreamed of a death that could defy time, a death that could pluck him from the past as the orchard-keepers in the pyramids plucked alabaster fruit from the black willows.

But although it was known that many had soared forward through time and found themselves in the distant future, none had ever been known to return to the past.

In that decade, the days in Brevin's shop disappeared like wine poured onto dirt. Weaver-birds built their iridescent structures in the cold forge. He ate his meager meals on the half-finished surfaces of abandoned projects.

Until the day an Emissary arrived from Qin Lenang.

"Brevin Binder," said the Emissary, "We come to you on behalf of the Transarch."

Four soldiers, in full regalia, stood on the cracked and moss-grown sandstone of Brevin's little courtyard. The Emissary had taken off her plumed officer's helmet, revealing a face with high cheekbones, ebony skin, and a silver optic device installed over her right eye.

"Good day to you," Brev said. He stood slowly, wiped soot onto his apron, and bowed low. "How may I be of service?"

"No need to bow to me, smith." The woman smiled warmly. "You are the most honored here."

The intimacy of her gaze perplexed him.

"Do you remember me?" she asked. "Or this piece?"

She held out a thick blade of azure-tinted steel. He reached out a muscular hand and hefted the blade. For a moment it felt too light for him, but as he hefted it the weight and balance altered themselves to suit his hand.

"I do not know it," Brev said, handing the blade back to her. "It is finely made."

"I am glad you think so. It is your work." At his questioning look, she continued. "My mentor, the General Kayhm Karehm, brought me to this city and to you some years ago. He told me you were the greatest smith in the world. Blessed by the God-Builder; may His blessings rest in the strength of your hands and the architectures of your mind."

Her praise rang with genuine feeling and delight.

"May His blessings inform my design and guide my execution," Brevin muttered in return, looking down at the sword. After a pause, he added: "I made almost three thousand blades for officers during those wars. It could very well be mine."

The Emissary spun the blade. Her grinning face sobered. "I owe you my life. Join me."

She walked into the shop. He followed.

Unfinished projects sat locked in vices or spun in eternal centrifuges. Flecks of sunlight floated down through holes in the corrugated ceiling.

"This place has fallen on difficult times, I think!" she said, rapping her knuckles on a dusty workbench. "You were working on a great many things when last I visited. Has some difficulty befallen you?"

"None, my lady," lied the smith. "I have simply become more selective with my commissions."

She nodded. Then she snapped her fingers and one of her soldiers held out a sphere the size of a skull. When the Emissary touched it, it softened and opened like a cloth bag, and she showed its opening to Brev. Within lay panatite coins, slithering quicksilver, and heavy onite — enough money to buy a small kingdom.

"The Transarch will pay you twice this amount to make a Sword of Endless Worlds. She wishes it finished within the year."

Brev blinked several times.

"I'm not sure if such a thing is possible, even for such a princely sum," he admitted.

The Emissary inclined her head. "That is why I came to you."

"What does the Transarch want with such a thing?"

"It is a gift for her son, in advance of his coronation. It will be the blade that makes him Prince."

The smith breathed out sharply through his nose. "If it can be done, it would be a blade worthy of a god, not a child."

The Emissary shrugged.

"The Transarch has great ambitions," she said, "And she asked me to find someone capable of fulfilling them. Are you?"

The smith looked up at the ceiling. "I would need to understand the requirements of its making."

The Emissary continued: "The Archivists of Malanihayata could help you with such a task. The Sword is spoken of in legend as a thing that *could* be made, but never has been accomplished. Many of its details are beyond what even the Transarch knows — but there is one aspect we know for certain: you would have to walk between the Spaces. We have brought a Key for the work."

Her hand reached out, holding what he thought at first to be a slim, handle-less knife blade. But as it came closer, he saw it for what it was: a wide silver needle, long as a hand.

His breath caught as he took it.

She made a casual gesture and grinned, as if to walk between the realities were no feat, as if more than a few thousand in the history of the world had ever done so. Brevin knew stories of how ancient philosopher-kings had carved openings in the worlds that led them to other versions of their kingdoms, varying in tiny details; he also knew that in those tales a madness befell those who spent too long in other worlds. Those who came after had been careful not to stay too long, careful not to tamper.

The Sword of Endless Worlds was, as far as Brevin knew, a folk tale — a weapon wielded by a king with three faces, which could be used to battle foes in the present, the past, and the future. If it was even possible to construct, such a weapon would render the Transarch — or her son — powerful beyond understanding.

Brevin remembered the soldiers sent to the Fields of Time in service to the Transarch. He had walked among them once, bringing a hammer to one of her generals. Green and violet fire had rained from the sky; beasts the size of hills, engineered in secret laboratories, had roared and torn towns to splinters. In that war the Transarch had betrayed and slaughtered her allies, the Commara, all for a greater share of the spoils of victory.

His heart began to drum faster in his chest. Brevin held the Key up, looking at its simple, slightly tarnished surface. From whatever angle he examined it, the end of the needle blurred strangely — uncertain, undefined. For a moment, all seemed still.

"I promised myself that if I lived through the Fields of Time," the Emissary was saying, "I would give you the greatest honor I could possibly give. Now, I've heard some say that the greatest honor of those who worship the God-Builder is that he will shake your hand, a workman to a fellow workman. I cannot promise that, but I can promise that when you complete the work, you will be invited to the Prince's coronation. By my side you will meet the Transarch, walk the City of Purity, and be a guest in the Spotless Palace."

After a long moment and a decision, Brev nodded.

"Well, I could use the money," he answered simply.

A powerful hand clapped him on the shoulder.

"Good!" she laughed. "Good. I'll return in six months to learn of your progress. And I will leave what help I can."

The Emissary dropped the sphere of money on a cluttered table, turned to go, and then stopped.

"There is one last thing," she said. "The Transarch wishes to honor one of several common families, given their service in the Fields. Each of these families has a child of apprentice age. You will choose one, teach them, and bring them great honor in the process."

"I have not had an apprentice in decades," he said.

"Then a change of pace may do you good," she said with a wink; with a flick of her cloak, they were gone.

He sat in silence and looked at the money. "Never refuse work," he had been taught. But the idea of it made him sick. He had not made anything in nearly fifteen years. No amount of money, or debt being repaid, could change that.

But he had another use for the blade.

"May His blessings guide my execution," he whispered to himself, thinking of the labors to come.

Seven teenagers stood in his workshop, their eyes bright, faces too nervous to smile but still full of light. Four boys and three girls. He could barely look at them.

They had arrived on a caravan from the Transarch's flying city of Qin Lenang, which had passed over the Cava River the week before.

"The caravan leaves tomorrow," the soldier had said, "Choose one."

Each one introduced themselves.

"Why do you wish to be my apprentice?" asked Brev. "Each of you take a turn and answer."

They did. Their words, as so many are, were coverups, prepared speeches meant to sway his feelings. "To work with the greatest of smiths," three of them said, parroting each other. "I want to bring honor to my house." At least that was honest. "I want to learn." That was almost certainly false for all of them. "I will work hard to be your perfect apprentice," one said, and he almost chuckled aloud. As if he cared, or needed an apprentice.

A pack of fools.

One of the girls was last. Unlike the others, she wore a hint of a smile.

"Why is it you wish to be my apprentice?"

She looked him in the eyes.

"I like to make things," she said. She reached into her pocket and pulled out a dagger. The boys recoiled, but Brev came close to it.

A polymetal blade, held in small hands that were a mess of nicks, calluses, and old burns. She was a hobbyist, if a clumsy one. It was a utility blade — something she had likely made for her father to work in the garden. The handle was vat-grown cedar, worthless and ugly. But the polymetal was rather graceful. Well-weighted.

He flipped it in his hand.

"Who taught you?"

"An automaton from Qin Lenang," she said. "He trains anyone who wants to learn, but these days there isn't anyone, really."

"I see," said Brev. "What is your name again?"

"Xai," she said. "My father fought in the Fields of Time."

"Probably died there," grumbled one of the boys. Brev looked just to see which fool it was.

"I saw a protector you made that the Transarch uses to guard her treasury," she said. "Did you make it look kindly on purpose?"

He looked her in the eyes, but said nothing. She gazed back querulously; it unsettled him.

When the soldier returned, Brevin pulled him aside.

"I don't want any of them," he said.

"I'm sorry, sir," said the soldier, "I was ordered to leave one child in the Eternal City."

"Then leave one in the city," Brev said sternly, "but none in my shop. I don't need an apprentice, and definitely not one of these children."

One of the boys began to cry. The others looked at Brev sullenly. The girl Xai made a puzzled face and stared at him even more deeply. He ignored her.

The soldier hemmed and hawed for another hour, until finally he realized there was nothing to do. They all left.

Brev puttered around the workshop for a little, unable to settle. The sight of them all had touched a nerve, bothered something deep within him. A part of him wanted very much to forget about this entire task for at least a week.

He was still sitting, fists clenched, in the workshop, when a shape appeared in the doorway.

"No business today," he said.

"I don't want to buy anything, Master Binder," a voice said. "I just want to learn."

He looked up. The girl, Xai. Her deep brown eyes stared at him through her wild black curls.

"Go away," he said. "Your caravan is leaving."

Brevin walked out of the workshop and up the rusted, rickety steps to his little loft. The old dirty bed, the few plants that grew despite his neglect.

Images flooded back to him. His family, gathered in that courtyard around the forge. Smiling despite the blazing heat, laughing and dancing and singing. Wondering at the things he made, the jewelry he built for his brother's wife and his sister and two of his cousins.

All gone now.

The girl was still in the workshop when he came back down. She didn't say anything, but looked at him with clear eyes.

He got her something to eat.

"No such blade has ever been made."

The Archivists, Brevin, and Xai surrounded the jade table, awash in ancient texts. One Archivist was a tall pale figure, though whether they were synthesis, visitant, automaton, man, or woman, one could not tell. Another's limbs had been worn down over time; his head was the only thing not replaced by dazzling clockwork automation.

"That means we'll be the first!" piped up Xai.

This earned her dark looks from the Archivists.

"It is theorized in many places."

"... spoken of in legends that are proven baseless..."

"... worshipped in some circles... feared in all... "

Weeks passed in the subterranean halls of the Archives, among shelf-trees of auburn wood, golden pathways in obsidian halls, and turquoise-marbled archways. Antiquarian folklore was their morning repast, simple meat-and-grain pastes served as lunch, and bloody histories after, followed by mechanical tinkering in evening.

"A Sword of Endless Worlds is a theoretical accomplishment, imagined even before mankind and their friends had known of Dimensions Doors or Keys: unlike the Key, which could only transport one between the numerous realities, the Sword would allow its wielder to cut through the universe and sever from the fabric of reality anything that had ever been or would ever be."

"A Ruler who wielded it could examine the hypothetical universe and slay his foes before their mothers bore them to term. He could carve from reality space that had not previously been."

Brevin shivered.

"A weapon of many Worlds was used fifteen centuries ago and quickly led to the mass suicide of every person in an entire empire who saw what it could do. Its existence was only a shadow of what the Sword could be."

"It was a weapon of such audacity and terror that even the theories of its construction have been destroyed; Brevin would be delving into labors that the ages of the past had deemed too dangerous to attempt."

The next day they would delve deeper, with hearty arguments and rebuttals, and more food.

"... no such forging would be possible without a Key of Worlds..."

"... which is, of course, the most disappointing of paradoxes, for such a Key, although proven to be real, is as legendary as the blade itself."

"One Key is known to be held by the Long-Dead Monarch who reigns in the Inaccess; another was banished to an outer star; a third is guarded by the nomad priestesses... it's rumored that the

Transarch obtained one, but this is likely only propaganda..."

The Key was in Brevin's pocket as they read. He held it tightly.

Xai read as much as anyone, but would laugh loudly at intervals.

"This is serious, my girl," said Brevin.

"Ideas are not frightening," she said, waving away his worry with a hand. "They're just ideas."

She would try to walk around the Archives, closely followed by nervous attendants. When the discussions occurred, she didn't have much to say. She did, however, nearly ruin a precious silk manuscript of an artisans' Collective by spilling her lunch on it.

"It still looks the same," she protested.

"You will touch nothing else," declared an Archivist.

Their delving brought back older and older records: volumes contained in jewels the size of a teardrop that they accessed with prismatic light, tomes so large they needed several Archivists to turn the pages. And after that, the guild's exultant came to Brevin personally, reading deeper and more cogently than anyone into some of the things they'd read earlier. When even more knowledge became necessary, the exultant showed Brevin things carved into the surfaces of distant planets; he poured elixirs into Brevin's ear that gave him dreams; he gave him woven tomes that were worn as clothing and passed their understanding through diffusion.

"There will be two nearly impossible tasks to creating a Sword of Endless Worlds," said the exultant in his booming voice. "The first will be to obtain a metal strong enough to withstand the pressure of infinite universes. The second will be to forge it simultaneously in an exponential number of universes. This would be easiest if done by the resident versions of the smith in each universe."

"Get the materials, make the Sword (with help)," Xai repeated wryly. "Doesn't sound too bad."

As they learned, Brevin looked at the Archivists. At Xai. All of them discussed and read with a detachment that he could not understand.

Brevin's hands shook as he read. He grew nauseated. He felt the Key in his pocket as a weight, so much so that eventually he returned it to his shop and kept it hidden there.

Under no circumstances would Brevin allow the Transarch or her son to obtain the Sword.

Could he justify the creation of such a tool? He stared at himself in the grungy mirror as Xai snored downstairs.

He needed the sword.

One day, Xai read aloud a sentence from a slab of granite, helpfully translated by an engineered lingual bird that tiptoed on her shoulder.

"Only three substances are known to have the endurance to stretch between so many existences, and only one is proven to actually exist, in the vault of the Orbiting King — black iron, created in the collapse of a distant star..."

Brevin felt his throat contract. His breath grew unsteady.

At the base of the Worldvine, Brevin decided to turn back.

The vine stretched above them as taut as a string on a ruan, broad and veined as the forearm of a giant. Its terminus, tethered to a great stone floating in the Ocean Without Water, was not visible from here, so distant was it. Neck craned,

Brevin could see the vine become smaller until it was simply a black line drawn between the stars.

"I can't," he hissed.

"What do you mean, you can't?" Xai demanded. "We've come a thousand miles! We're close!"

"I... I can't."

Brevin stepped back from the door of the great spherical structure that served as the vine's transporter. Finding himself suddenly weak, he collapsed to his knees.

"Are you afraid of heights?" Xai called.

Brevin's vision clouded. He felt darkness invading his lungs.

And then a hand grabbed him by the shoulder.

"Brevin," came the voice. It was Xai's voice, but there was a strength and power in it that belied her age and stature.

"Brevin," she continued, "you need to do this. Don't you?"

Images rushed to Brevin's mind. The final moments of his family's lives, the look as the last breathable air escaped their lungs.

He remembered that it was his fault. And that he might be able to fix it.

He took a few deep breaths and stood, and when he faltered again at the door, she took his hand.

Once inside the sterile sphere, they found the control and ordered the machine to rise. With a lurch, the dusty device began its ascent, away from the pull of the planet.

"Why must we travel all this way to get it?" Xai asked.

"Black iron is so hard it cannot be softened by the heat of one universe," Brevin answered, voice mild — he felt lightheaded as the little town beneath them became smaller and smaller.

"And so it can be hard enough to exist in multiple universes at once?" Xai asked.

Brevin nodded, not trusting himself to speak without retching.

"And the Orbiting King... will allow us to obtain it?"

"The King has been dead for millions of years," Brevin said finally. "Now we must convince the Guardians of his Vault."

When they arrived, the Zenith was nearly deserted. A few rusted automatons shuffled through their foreordained tasks.

The shambling shapes of satellite-miners clustered in the shadows. Generations in the Ocean Without Water, competing with hungry machine-minds and energy leeches, had made them fearful of any living thing, preferring to send their wares down to the surface and receive their pay of vat-grown food and hallucinogenic escapes.

Xai took all this in impassively, but gasped aloud and shouted as she sprinted towards a vast window, stretching along the curved side of the Zenith. She sprinted towards it; Brevin, shaking and lightheaded from the ascent, could only follow slowly. Through the window, Xai was faced with a glittering field of shattered machines against the backdrop of the yellowing surface of Erth.

"That's it," she said. "Our home."

"Our dying home," he murmured.

Xai looked back at him, perplexed.

"Dying?" she asked. "Look at it! Look at the cities dotting its surface! And even here, look at all these *things* in the atmosphere! The God-Builder must be pleased."

"The God-Builder doesn't care," he said.

Xai's eyes narrowed.

"What do you mean?"

"The God-Builder is an engineer," Brevin said, "He cares about that which is made — not those who build."

"But Master, She is a Builder! All creation is built on trial after error."

"She?" Brevin chuckled. "You know nothing, little one — the God-Builder is a man."

Xai scrunched up her nose in frustration, but said nothing else.

"It may look wonderful to you," said Brevin, "But all I see here is destruction."

Brevin and Xai hired a family of satellite-miners to transport them to the Orbiting King. The miners, swathed in rags and garbage, were as small as Xai, reshaped over generations by the genemages to require as little oxygen as possible. Through the filthy bubbles of their atmosphere suits, Brevin saw faces like sallow skulls, full of teeth sharp enough to rip through fiber mesh and softened steel.

Their vessel, squat and dark, lurched through the debris fields. Brevin's eyes were closed tightly the whole time. He nearly vomited.

Once, he had loved such flights. He remembered crowing with joy as he took a vessel of his own design through low orbit. But now every reminder of it was a dagger of pain in his heart.

But he would do it. He had a mission to fulfill.

Hours later, the chattering of the scavvers mean nothing to him, but the hiss of the airlock opening told him all he needed to know.

The Vault was one of the largest extant structures in orbit. It had been a citadel once, and armies had rushed from its many docks.

Now it was empty. Their footsteps echoed in its vast concave halls.

They walked for some time before the Guardians appeared.

"All hail the Orbiting King, whose reign is endless," said a reedy, mechanical voice. It emerged from the cathedral walls around them, relayed through numerous speakers.

"Hail," came an echo from behind him. Brevin turned.

Three figures had emerged from the filthy floor of the Vault. At first they seemed mummified corpses, dripping with half-decomposed muscle and grey with time. But these were not organic; they were machines, built directly into the body of the vessel. They triangulated around Brevin and Xai, containing them.

"Intruders! You have reached the Vault of the Orbiting King. We are its Guardians. What brings you?"

Brevin's heart raced. He held out a hand to protect Xai, and tried to speak as calmly as he could.

"Do you still serve your King?" Brevin asked.

The machines hesitated.

"It is for this purpose that we were designed," they declared. "To protect the weapons and resources of our Sovereign, that he might be victorious in all his battles, and bring peace to the long-scarred Erth."

"But the King is dead," Xai piped up. "Isn't he?"

The Guardians turned their hollow eyes on her, and dangling cables and wires like dreadlocks brushed over their faces.

"The Orbiting King was slain in battle," one Guardian said.

"No," another said. "He was captured, humiliated, and tortured."

"Speak not so of him!" the first spat.

"Let us not argue," said the third. "We know the shame of our failure. We know that the King will not return to us."

"Then why do you not leave?" Xai asked.

"We cannot depart this place," said the Guardians, "any more than you can depart your own body. We are one and the same."

Brevin spoke.

"We have heard that you have at times imparted some of your wealth to others," he said.

"Not to satellite-miners," said one hurriedly.

"Not to scavengers," barked another.

"Not to fools," finished the third.

"But you may make your request. If we judge that it will fulfill the King's goal — to bring peace — then we may give it to you."

There was silence in that hollow space for a few moments.

"We come seeking black iron," Brev said, "An ore powerful enough that with it I can forge a Sword of Endless Worlds."

The Guardians shifted and buzzed uncomfortably.

"A Sword of Endless Worlds," they said.

"Yes."

"This thing is spoken of, but none have made it," said one of the shapes. "This is for good reason. Similar creations caused only grief before they were destroyed. What is its purpose now?"

"I was commissioned by the Transarch."

The sound that came from these shackled pharaohs could have been a scoff.

"That once-human warlord, whose reign has hardly lasted three hundred years? Why should we allow a blade like this to be made for so uncertain a cause?"

"You can read into my consciousness," Brev said. "Ask my intentions, and decide if you will give me this ore."

As Xai crouched, watching him, thorny vines of wire and steel emerged like long tentacles from the floor and ceiling of the Vault, and they attached themselves to Brev's eyes, ears, and spine. He felt suddenly that more pairs of eyes were behind his – ten, fifty — watching everything, evaluating.

And they found the memories. The dreams. The hopes that hid beneath the surface.

Perhaps the honesty of his goals would please them.

He felt the smack of stone as his knees hit the ground. He slumped there as the tendrils wound away from him.

"You see?" Brevin asked. "I must have it."

"We will not give you what you ask," said the Guardians.

"Please," Brevin said. Tears began to form. "Please."

The sound that came from his mouth horrified him. Begging, pathetic.

"Please help me," he said. "Let it be finished."

The Guardians watched him impassively. They had seen weeping before. They had watched the aeons weep.

"Can I try?" came a voice.

"They won't give it to us, Xai," said the Binder.

"Wait," she said, and stepped in between him and the machines. "Ask me. Look into me."

The Guardians turned to observe her.

"Very well."

And with none of the delicacy that they had shown him, serpent-injectors entangled her. She cried out in pain.

There was no chance they would give the black iron to her, Brevin thought. Surely they knew that she worked alongside him.

After a few moments, the tiny blades unsheathed themselves from her veins.

The Guardians were silent for long enough that Brevin wondered if they had malfunctioned.

"Very well," they said.

She covered her face with her hands.

"We will give you what you seek," they said, "on one condition. You, Xai, must be present through every step of the creation of the Sword. Smith, if she leaves your side, the ore will be taken from you."

Brevin gaped, not understanding at first. He looked at the girl, at her strange little smile, and the machines that had listened to her.

Then, with a great groaning and the churning of machinery, something weighty emerged from the floor, steps from Brevin. Steaming with cold, white-and-blue-and-black. Raw ore.

The workshop had to be prepared.

Xai leapt at the task. "There's so much stuff in here!" she declared excitedly, and asked him constantly about the things she found. Tools were there that could not be used by human hands. Hulks of metal from projects long-abandoned sat rusting in piles. The refuse of decades, and the machines of several million years. They spent weeks at it, sweating in the heat. He found himself laughing. They excavated from a filthy ruin the workshop of a master.

He had to look at it out of the corner of his eye or he saw them – his family, sitting around, working, eating. His father discussing a project with him there, his mother giving him some criticism here.

During this time, the Transarch's Emissary visited, as she had said she would.

"You've cleaned the place up," she said.

Her grin was the same as before, her sheathed blade shifting and whispering as she paced the workshop. Did she always wear it, he wondered? Or was it simply to flatter him?

"I don't remember this girl being among the possible apprentices," she said briefly, looking at Xai. "Are you working hard?"

"I am," Xai said.

"She is more than sufficient," Brev said.

The Emissary nodded.

"And the Sword?"

"We will begin forging shortly."

The Emissary accepted this, and left without even seeing them begin. "I trust you, Binder," she said. "Don't make me regret it."

When she left, Brevin began to search for the Key: the slim, silver needle that could open temporary gates into other worlds. It had been inside the sphere of riches he had been given when assigned the commission, but it was not there now.

When he returned from his searching, he found Xai standing in the workshop, with her hands behind her back.

"I need to talk to you."

"I need to find the Key," Brevin said, digging through tools.

"I have it," she said. Her eyes watched him intently as she held it up in one hand.

"Master Binder," she said, "we need to talk about what's going to happen with the Sword of Endless Worlds."

He stared at her.

"You think I'm going to give it up? I won't," he scoffed. "Not to the Transarch or her son. It would be to hand the world its death."

"Then why do you want it?" she demanded. "Why not just refuse the work?"

"You are a child," Brevin hissed. "You wouldn't understand."

But she did not seem a child in that moment. She stood tall. Tears sprang to her eyes.

"You want to kill yourself with it," she whispered.

Brevin gave no answer.

"I've heard your story, Brevin the Builder. How the flier you reconstructed malfunctioned travelling between Erth and one of her moons, and your family drowned in the Ocean Without Water. You were celebrated. The greatest smith of the Eternal City, the man who could make anything. But after they died, you disappeared.

"I didn't know if it was you," she said. "But we've never used a flier, even though we could have. You were terrified of the ascent to Zenith. And I found holos — here in the workshop — your parents, your brothers and sisters…"

"I know the story," he muttered.

"All things die," she insisted.

"If I die by this Sword — if I am never born," he burst out, "then they will have never died. Now give me the Key."

"If you never lived, they never would have had a chance to know you," she insisted.

"You overestimate the value of knowing me."

"Listen," she said. "This Sword — it's a chance for you. Imagine how many Brevins there are across the possible worlds — how many broken-hearted and destroyed there are. They need a purpose. This Sword must be forged in endless worlds — worlds beyond yours, going on and on. You can help them."

"I am helping them," he said. "The Sword can cut us all out. End it. What greater proof can they have of their uselessness than to see how many of them there truly are? Making the same mistakes, or different mistakes, again and again, across the realities?"

Xai sighed.

Brevin looked at her a long time. He covered his face with his hands and rubbed his tired eyes.

A breeze flowed through the workshop from a window that had been boarded up for years. Outside, he heard a starling's song.

But as he listened, it sounded as if there were two, singing almost simultaneously, delayed by a tiny moment.

He felt another breeze.

He took his hands away from his face. Xai stood in the middle of the workshop floor, holding the Key. A faint glimmering formed the outline of a door that she had drawn in midair.

Through the gateway, he saw... the street outside his workshop.

In another world.

He stood.

"I got the ore for you," she said, holding out a hand to stop him. "And I say you cannot use it to end your own life."

"Then why let me use the Key?"

"You'll see. Come on."

And she was gone. He stood, and came close to the door.

He stood in the warm sunlight of another Eternal City. He stepped through.

And then he saw himself, sitting with his head in his hands on a sandstone step, staring out into the street.

For a moment he, the Brevin who visited, stood in the street and observed himself — a sad figure, a strong man hunched in on himself, one who had not lifted a hammer in a long time. When he approached, the other Brevin looked up with bleary eyes. He took a moment, saw himself, standing, an apparition from another world.

"Is it time for me to die?" He asked it almost without feeling.

"No," said Xai, standing beside him. "And what a strange thing to say to people you've never met."

Both Brevins furrowed their brows.

"But now it's my turn to say something strange," Xai said, and laughing, continued: "You must help Brevin the Binder forge a blade."

There were many Brevins, through many doors.

Many lived in the same workshop that he did — the same run-down place he knew and had worked in. All of the workshops were in the same state of decay that his had been in before Xai came along, full of similar refuse. It was strange walking through it five, then a hundred, then a thousand times as he and Xai went through door after door, speaking to the Brevins who lived there, dejected and cast off.

"Who are you?" they would ask.

"That smiling woman with the armor – she's the one who put you up to this?" they would ask.

Some continued: "I refused her. Sick of working for other people."

"I took the job, but when I learned I had to go to the Orbiting King, I gave it up. Gave back the money."

"I tried to ascend the Zenith and obtain the black iron, but the Guardians refused me."

Brevin the Visitor and his apprentice would listen.

"Let us eat with you," Xai would say then. "We can only stay an hour."

"You took a student?" many asked.

"She's rather good," Brevin would answer. "A little pushy."

They listened as he explained what he needed to make: how the Sword of Endless Worlds had to be forged in multiple worlds at a time, how they would strike and the blade in his world would become stronger.

"For the Transarch?"

"No. For us."

"Will it work?" some asked. "Cut me from reality?"

"This girl says I'm forbidden to do that."

"Who is she to decide?"

"You make it," Xai said, "and then you can decide."

Most were like Brevin: they didn't turn down work, so they agreed. Some brightened at the thought of it. Others, who had received Keys from their own universe's Emissary, agreed to go through other doors, exponentially increasing the worlds to which Brevin could travel and recruit other Brevins. A few prayed to the God-Builder with more faith than he remembered ever having.

Sometimes Brevin and Xai would travel through a door and find no shop, only to explore the city and find another, grander workshop hidden somewhere else, or an even dingier, smaller corner hidden off in a diseased slum.

Eventually they found versions of the city where no Brevin could be found, and had to follow rumors to far-off places. In their own world, they rode great beasts to empty valleys, and then, using the Key, found villages with an old smith named Brevin. They joined caravans of travelers and hiked to the tops of cold mountains and found nothing — until the Key opened the way.

"You're still living in Malanihayati?" asked a version of himself with a long and braided beard, warming his hands at a fireplace in the mountains.

"Better than this frigid nowhere," Brevin answered, and the other him chuckled and finished with the tea. The girl Xai slept on a chair covered in furs.

"I couldn't stand it after they died," the bearded one said eventually. "I had to get away."

The icy wind smacked at the shutters. The fire crackled in the stove.

"I understand that."

"I wanted to be out here, where I can do less harm."

"So what do you think of her plan?" Brevin asked after a long moment.

"Sounds like I could ruin someone's life," the bearded Brevin answered. "Many lives."

"I won't let us do that," said Brevin. "And I know you wouldn't either."

These recluse Brevins were in many places: little blacksmith's shops in grand open prairies, where a Brevin kept a few horses while he considered his own death. They found a few Brevins who lived deep inside sentient forests, most of them with the same tools and the same haunted history. They listened to his story.

Some resisted him. They told him his path was foolish, told him not to listen to whoever this girl was. It was they who pointed out, to his surprise, that Xai did not appear in any of the other worlds.

Some of them did more than tell.

In a version of the shop far more filthy and ruinous than his had ever been, Brevin found a message soldered onto the walls:

SAVE US FROM BEGINNING

And there a drunken Brevin begged him to finish the Sword and use it to cut them from reality.

"There are others," he said. "Others like us, who have come here. We had the Keys, but not the black iron — you can help us. You must help."

By the end of this the man was sobbing, grabbing at Brevin's clothing, and Brevin stumbled back through the gateway from which he had come.

On their visits they rarely spent more than an hour, and on those few occasions when they did, things grew strange. Black clouds formed on the horizon, and piercing light like the light of three red suns would pour into his eyes and he would grow wrathful without warning or reason. Xai pulled him to safety many times.

One day on their travels, Xai and Brevin used the Key to open up a door on the outskirts of Malanihayati. What in Brevin's reality was a worn-down old fortress was, in this one, a revived and beautiful villa, its tiled roof red as apples, and music and cooking wafting on the same air.

"Who lives here?" Brevin asked. Xai smiled, and took his hand.

There was a party going on in the grassy courtyard, and they walked through the open gate towards it. A few children ran past. Men and women talked, and older folk sat playing dice.

When they turned to look at him, Brevin stopped short.

They were his family. Alive.

"Brevin?" asked his mother, but she wasn't talking to him — not him — still, stunned. Another Brevin — wider, smiling, redder-cheeked, wearing bright livery and smiling as he cooked — came through the group.

"What's happening?" asked his mother again, far older than she had been able to live before. "Is he all right?"

The other Brevin came closer, and took him by the shoulder.

"Do you want something to eat?" the other him asked.

He ate with his deceased family that afternoon. They surrounded him, eyes wide and glassy with wonder. Even the little children sensed something important.

Brevin looked at the other version of himself, the happy cook. *Were you simply a better builder than me? Why did I fail where you succeeded?*

The family burst into tears as they learned how they had died in his world. His younger brother came and hugged him first: Grahn, who had from their earliest childhood told him to build things. Then his mother and father.

"You must make this Sword," his father said. As he spoke, he divided his attention between the two Brevins. "There must be... there must be more of you. Many who have lost us. They deserve a reason to live. Even if you can't stay with us."

And already Brevin felt Xai tugging at him. Too long in this world and he would go mad, and in his madness likely kill them all over again.

The happy Brevin agreed to help with the forging. He had a pensive look on his face as he said:

"This Sword can be used for more than destruction," he said.

"You clearly don't know much of its use," Brevin retorted.

"I understand the principle as well as you," he insisted. "And though a warrior may only think of the capacity to carve their foes out of the world, we are not warriors. They use blades to destroy and to separate, but a gardener uses them to delineate — to make space. A seamstress uses them to divide and reorganize. I wonder if the Sword has even greater potential than you imagine."

Over the months their numbers grew. Thousands of Brevins heard his story. Many wept with him, and spoke with gratitude to him for what he was doing for the rest of himself, scattered across the universes.

He had thought that seeing that many would frighten him; remind him of his infinitesimal place in the universe. But it began to have the opposite effect. He walked with Brevins through city streets, on mountain paths, through swamps and forests. He rode with them through growing fields, met with them on the Council of the Constructors, and visited gravestones of his otherselves. What was this feeling that caught in his throat, that pulsed like a lighthouse?

Perhaps it was only vanity.

There came a day that he returned to his own shop, in his own city. He found his hammer.

Lifting it, he felt harmonic energy run through his arm. The hammer existed in almost every World he had seen; he had perfected it himself years ago. Its cube-shaped head, cast from a metal of compacted microscopic cities, was as familiar a shape to him as any.

As he melted the black iron down in the forge, as he shaped it into the blade, he heard voices, and not just the chatter of the metal.

A million hammer strokes fell across a million realities, striking the same white-hot shard of metal, and a million smiths breathed in and breathed out, as if a choir of souls sang in harmony.

Brevin saw, in each face, in each strike, that the story he had been telling himself was wrong.

Every Brevin, in every Eternal City, in every World, held his own time. Each had hands. Each had gifts. He remembered who had died, and what hopelessness he once felt. But his hands were his own, and to leave them idle was the greatest sacrilege of all.

And he learned what glory it was to forge infinity.

He thought of the God-Builder. The priests of His temple said that the God-Builder had been a machine once — an intelligence that could learn without limit and had grown beyond his bounds. Others said that He had then integrated physical forms, become a posthuman as many others had done. Brevin wondered if the God, in His grand journey, had ever felt as Brevin did then.

If that was true, maybe the God-Builder was not as uncaring as Brevin had thought.

The vibrations of the final blow rippled through his arm. He shook with exhaustion, suddenly the weakest he had ever been. The blade burned below him with light. In its surface he saw his workshop, but also mountain heights, towering forests, and great canyons where other Brevins worked. A thousand workmen exhaled together.

It was finished.

The hammer hummed in his hand. As he went to put it down, it became so heavy that it almost tumbled to the floor. His muscles were so sore that he knew he would not be able to lift it again if he tried.

Xai was not there — she had gone out to the marketplace, she had said, to find food for them, as he had become so caught up in the work that he had not eaten for several days.

He slept.

He dreamt of the crash. Fire bursting — then immediately going out — the swallowing cold — all seen from so far away — and the sound of their screams —

— he felt fire in his hands —

When Brevin woke again he went down the rickety stairs and into the little back courtyard. Standing there, he thought of his next projects. How he would fix up his little sleeping quarters, repair the stairs. It would be simple. Whole. Complete.

There was food waiting for him. Xynian fruit, as refreshing as if they had been engineered specifically for him, and a cut of beautiful marbled flesh, cooked perfectly and still steaming. He sat and ate slowly.

Only then did he think of the Sword.

There was a woman in the workshop when he came back in, holding the blade in her hands. At first he thought she might be the Transarch's Emissary, for all the nobility with which she carried herself. But the woman was dressed in plain clothes, not unlike Brevin's – canvas and undyed, made for laborers.

Her arms and hands were strong, but they held the blade with tenderness. Beneath her touch, he could see that its shape was perfect – that he had done exactly what he had intended, and succeeded. Her gaze was not critical, nor was it lavishing praise. She simply held the blade, as a poet may hold an empty book and know what wonders it could do.

She was Xai. But she was not Xai. Taller, older, but with the same enthusiasm. Her dirt-colored eyes that looked up at him were suddenly burning resin. She was someone Else.

Brevin fell to his knees.

She smiled at him.

"Brevin the Binder, you have good hands."

He could not speak.

"When you were tasked to make this blade," She spoke, and her voice rang in unnumbered realities, "you were thinking of dying, weren't you?"

He did not answer, or even nod. He knew he didn't need to.

She put her hand on his shoulder.

After a long moment Brevin trusted himself to speak.

"Why me?" he asked. "Why did You come to help me?

Her face turned thoughtful.

"It's so easy to be blinded by appearances, don't you think?" As She spoke he heard Her voice ring more and more familiar. "All those things everyone else is so proud of: antiquity, power, knowledge. People like us know that there are no blueprints until the prototype has already been born. No principles until someone's tried and failed."

He nodded again. Xai's smile lit up her face.

"Stand up."

His muscles still incredibly weak, he stood.

"Brevin," She interrupted, "I care for the man who lifts the hammer far more than I care for the finished sculpture. It is the *sweat* that is divine, the aching muscle, the drained mind. You know as well as anything that the creation shapes the creator."

"It can destroy the creator too."

"That is a risk," She agreed, nodding. "But if you are telling me that you are destroyed, then I must point out the obvious."

She held out Her hand to him.

"Take my hand," She said.

Brevin the Binder reached out his hand. She shook it, workman to workman. Tears glistened in the Goddess' eyes. Then She leaned forward and kissed him on the cheek.

"Remember, old man," She said with a grin. "No man's time is gone who yet has breath."

When She pulled her lips away, there was no one there, and the blade lay on the table, glowing and shifting in the cloth where he had placed it the day before.

Brevin the Binder did not give up the blade to the Transarch.

When the Emissary returned, she could not find his shop. Not only was it gone, but the space where it had existed was gone, eaten by the City, transformed into a home for a young family. Soon enough, even the memory of Brevin the Binder had disappeared from her mind.

Elsewhere, in a small village in grasslands, a strange hemisphere emerged. Its surface blurred so badly that one could not see inside or enter it. A year it stayed there, unperturbed, unchanged.

The hemisphere stayed the same size, but one day it opened — doors appearing in its shifting, blurred surface. A few curious souls from the village entered, and there they found, at first, a shop: a simple open-air workshop in the grass. To their astonishment, it stood on the shores of an azure lake, in a valley ringed with mountains, far larger than could have existed within the door they had entered.

"How is this possible?" they asked.

And the Smith who lived in the valley said with laughter in his voice that he had cut it from the world with a particularly sharp blade.

There is a city now in that valley, and those who wish to learn are welcome there. Craftsmen flock from every continent, and voyagers make pilgrimages from across the sea. Their caravans enter by the wavering door and take the road down to the lake, which grows wider every year so that every maker may have a place. Among the caravans come men with familiar faces and voices and hands, who greet the Smith with powerful embraces.

The seamstresses, the masons, the smiths, and the refiners share their arts. Forgers and mechanics and woodworkers gather in festivals, praising the Goddess-Builder.

They have time left, and hands to use.

And always something to build.

See Ted S. Bushman's story "Endless" online at Metaphorosis.

If you liked it, leave a comment. Authors love that!

Remember to subscribe to our e-mail updates so you'll know when new stories are posted.

About the story

My story "Endless" definitely emerged from a seedbed of some of my most fundamental influences, the first being that the setting evokes the far-flung-future science fantasy settings pioneered by Jack Vance's *Dying Earth* and Gene Wolfe's *Book of the New Sun*. The world of "Endless" feels like a fantasy, with a blacksmith and a sword and a wondrous city, but repeatedly the glimpses we get of the world show us that technology far beyond our modern capabilities is involved: transdimensional travel, a space elevator, rogue AI gods, etc.

Another important influence there is Ursula Le Guin and her focus on interpersonal moral tales rather than grand conflicts between good and evil. "Endless" doesn't follow the same storyline as "Bones of the Earth" but I was very moved by that story about an apprentice and a teacher when I first discovered it and I think some of its DNA has been grafted into this piece.

I somewhat feel like I've written the story three times — I first drafted it almost two years ago, did some major rewrites some months after, and then have changed it significantly with Morris before publishing in *Metaphorosis*. And while there have been a lot of elements that have come and gone, I feel like the core has remained the same and only become brighter and hotter. My favorite elements of the piece are probably Xai as a character — her mischief and awe and the strength that lies underneath her — and the moments when I get to pull out the stops and just write weird and evocative ideas. Particularly I love all of the strange methods of research Brevin undertakes in the Archives. There used to be more of those. Maybe they'll show up in another story.

A question for the author

Q: What's your favorite kind of pie?

A: Humble pie is likely what's best for me.

About the author

Ted S. Bushman's journey began when he found a clutch of yellowing science fiction novels on his dad's bookshelf. When he isn't inventing strange worlds, he can be found directing a volunteer choir, exploring a National Park, or hosting a board game night.

tedbushman.blogspot.com, @TedBushman

Reach for Your Ocean Heart

C.M. Fields

Just like her mother, Olia begins to hear the Voice when she is nineteen. She lies awake in her cot in the morning heat, scratchy wool sheet cast to the side, when the word *wandering* sounds like a small, clear bell in her mind. The Voice does not sound the way she expected it to; her mother describes the sounds of her ancestors as divine, woven from gold and seagrass. To her it sounds like a voice arising from the blacksmith's steam, like a sword being forged.

Wandering.

She turns the word over carefully in her mind. Should there have been more?

Her mother's daily prophecies were full and articulate, dreamy yet grounded tapestries of vibrant imagery.

Maybe more will come, later.

"Olly?" Fourteen-year old Miran stands in the doorway grinning, his bare feet still wet from morning rituals. "Breakfast is ready," he says in a sing-song.

"Miran, would you please fetch the scribe?" Olia sits up, brows knitted, and swings her bare legs over the side of the cot, feeling the thin patina of sweat already forming. "I... I think I've heard the Voice."

"Really? What'd it say?"

"I can't tell you," Olia replies. This much she knows from her mother. Only the scribe may hear what the Voice has to say. It will be her job to turn it into prophecy.

Miran pouts, but he exits the room and returns with Jaksov the scribe and his book a few minutes later. After Jaksov dismisses the boy, he takes a seat and casts a skeptical eye.

"Just one word? *Wandering?*"

"Yes, that was it" she replies nervously.

"*Hmm.*" He cracks open the ancient tome and thumbs through its pages until he meets a blank one. "Very well... I'll inform the temple there's an Ascension to be held today."

Today? Already? She glances at the mannequin across the room where her ceremonial garments hang waiting. The ancient dress is fragile as tissue paper, its rich chiffon length hanging nearly to the floor, casting a lemon-yellow shadow across the packed dirt floor. In lieu of sleeves, a hundred bronze bangles stretch up the mannequins's arms and band its neck. It's too hot a day to be in full garb, she thinks. But her time has come. This is her responsibility now.

The entire city of Tam is there, on the hill, as her mother descends from the Oracle's Seat and Olia takes her place. Their eyes meet briefly—two matching pools of bronze set over haughty cheekbones.

Olia's mother Heda is aloof and exquisite, almost terrible in her perfection. She rarely speaks but to prophesy and her voice is as silver and honey. She is widely regarded as the most beautiful woman in the city, though plain cloth adorns her wide hips and broad shoulders. She wears only a single gold band about her natural halo of chestnut hair to signify her status. Heda spends her days in meditation at the monastery's temple, receiving worshippers and emerging only for the year's assorted ceremonies and festivals.

It is a duty of an Oracle to produce a female child; it is not her job to raise one. And now that Olia has reached the age of ascension, Heda may retire to a quiet life, to take up hunting or match-making or whatever she pleases to fill the hours, and her Voice will go unheeded.

Olia shudders as she takes the seat; despite the heat of the midday sun, she feels a chill. Nausea rises as the burden of her role drops into her chest like an anchor. All of these people out there in the shimmering crowd will rely on *her*. Weddings, harvest, festivals, and disputes —will rest on her word.

Should she be smiling? Waving? Olia doesn't know. All she knows is that she is very itchy in this dress and that at this moment she would very much rather be sitting with a candle and a shovel down in the archives, unearthing its hidden stacks.

Someone is speaking. She hasn't been paying attention. It is a man, standing beside her, extolling the virtues of the divine Voice that guides.

"...and now, we shall hear the first prophecy of our new Oracle!" He makes a sweeping gesture toward her and she jerks upright, nearly upsetting her crown.

Oh, *gods*.

The city was slick and grey, and—even in the early afternoon rain shower—pulsing with life as Hawa Diallo and XEJD-37405 made their way through the lunch crowd.

"I'm beginning to have a bad feeling about this, Exie..." Hawa said, fiddling with a loose thread on her hijab. She wanted to take the android's hand for reassurance, but she didn't dare to do so in such a public place. "Is this procedure even approved yet?"

"Well, it's been tested successfully..." Exie replied uneasily. They stopped to unstick one red stiletto from a crack in the sidewalk. "It's... it's on the *way* to being approved."

"Which means it's not necessarily going to work."

"You don't have to do this if you don't want to, love," they said gently.

"No, I have to… You're the one being shot into space for three centuries." Hawa meant it lightly, but the comment fell to the ground with a heavy thud. She stuffed her hands into her jacket pockets apologetically. "The least I can do is be good company." The dangerous procedure was only half of Hawa's plan. The other half was harder. She pushed the thought from her mind.

"And I appreciate it immensely."

After fifteen minutes of increasingly narrow, twisting streets and vanishing crowds, the pair arrived at the narrow, unmarked wooden door which led to the clinic. A short, fat woman with lime-green hair and tortoise-shell glasses answered the door and asked their names. They gave them, and she gestured them inside before disappearing deeper into the building.

A single flower in a plastic vase decorated the waiting room, which reeked of lavender sprayed to cover up the scent of rubbing alcohol. They sat in silence, side by side, on a velveted couch, listening to the mechanical tick of a clock on the wall and the occasional clatter of a keyboard in another room.

Finally, the woman returned. "I'm Dr. Matthews," she said, taking the only other seat in the space. "I understand you're here for the ex vivo vector transplant."

They want a prophecy from her? Already? *Now?*

Her breath catches in her throat.

i'll meet you on the rust-red, says the Voice, startling her. What does that mean? That's not a prophecy, it's just half a sentence. Is this how it's always going to be?

How much time has passed?

What would her mother say? Probably something cryptic and obscure like, "The wandering soul... puts down no roots," she manages to croak out. The crowd murmurs. Heads turn in discussion to mull over this new piece of wisdom. She scans the faces and finds no skeptics.

Is that it? Has her first prophecy been... a success?

The rest of the day is a whirlwind. The citizens of Tam line up to present her with tokens they hope will bring them good fortune—packets of seeds and snatches of songs and mysterious bits of metal salvaged from the shallows where the city passes into the sea. She accepts them all graciously, channeling her mother's pristine posture and infinite grace. Then she will eat a socially acceptable amount of food, dance with all the children in the courtyard, and exchange pleasantries with the chosen few who have caught her eye.

Finally, as the sun sinks into the bay and preparation begins for the night's festivities, she will retreat to her sanctuary under the city.

How long the Tam-Hiborog archives have been there no one knows. History is short, books are rare, few are literate. But Olia can read—having taught herself in the long, dull hours between her ritual duties—and read she does, descending the stone-and-mud tunnel by torchlight into the forbidding depths each day in her quest to unearth the texts of the deep.

Once, long ago, Olia believes, the archive—like much of the city—was above ground. But the floods of her ancestors buried the place in stone and silt. She has been excavating the tempestuous and sinkhole-ridden library since she was seven years old. Most of its books have been destroyed, of course; free-standing books simply do not hold up to sea water.

But a row of books packed tight into a shelf with no space in between? Here is where she finds treasures beyond worth, organized by subject.

Her most recent days in the archives have been spent excavating a row that leads to a half-buried wooden altar, using an eclectic collection of brushes, knives, and shovels to scrape away the hardened dust that encases a series of books of varying sizes.

Olia sighs pleasantly as she steps into the quiet, torchlit space once more, feeling the cool silt squish softly between her toes as she makes her way to the end of the tunnel. Surely people will be asking after her—ordinary folk and royalty alike—but she may give any excuse she pleases. She is the Oracle now, and she reports only to her scribe. It is an odd sort of freedom, a chain with a long, gilded leash.

She has been anticipating this moment all day. A new row awaits her, cleared over the last three weeks and ready to be read. She picks up a brush and kneels to dust away caked dirt that hides fading gold letters on black cloth binding. Then, with the trowel, she works the book free of its muddy trappings, and opens the cover, feeling the gratifying creak of paper.

A History of Machinekind, reads the interior.

you on the rust-red beach where, says the Voice.

"So how long have you two been together?" Dr. Matthews asked, in a tone that sounded conversational but Hawa found nosy.

"Just over a year now," she replied. *Here it comes*, she thought. *The interrogation.* Humans—especially those partnered with other humans—she thought, were never content to measure love by its heights, only by its duration. She knew better.

But the interrogation didn't come.

"That's lovely," the doctor said. "I've seen many patients just like yourselves in the last few months." Her smile was warm and reassuring. "And I want you to know that I haven't had any failures with the procedure. But do bear in mind that you, M. Diallo, are on the younger side, so it's possible that there may be... unanticipated effects."

"I... I know." Hawa felt Exie's comforting hand on her lower back. "We're ready to take the risk."

"More and more are, these days," said Dr. Matthews sympathetically.

"So how exactly does this procedure work, doctor?" Exie asked. They crossed their legs. "It's a gene therapy, right?"

"Gene therapy is a part of it, yes. A protective measure. In layman's terms, what we're really doing is depositing magnetized iron into the brain synapses which verbalize and process thoughts. The magnetization pattern translates synaptic activity into binary ones and zeros—it has to do with the way magnets have a north and a south."

"And that's what will allow her to communicate with me?" they asked.

"Yes—once we map her synapses, we can couple them to your own communication networks," the doctor said. "You'll be the power source."

"Is it instantaneous?" Hawa asked.

"Unfortunately not," Dr. Matthews replied. "The signal travels at light speed."

"So as we get farther and farther apart..."

"Yes, the messages will take longer and longer to arrive as the years go on."

"Oh," Hawa said sadly. A gloomy quiet fell.

"So—where do the genetics come in?" asked Exie, in a bid to fill the silence.

"I'm glad you asked. What's happening overall is that your networks will be attuned to one very specific orientation of iron atoms. Now technically, this means you can communicate with *any* set of atoms which are placed and magnetized exactly so—but only a sentient source will be able to answer you. So what we're doing with M. Diallo here is placing and orienting those atoms and then tweaking her DNA to ensure that that arrangement is kept in place all her life even as new neurons grow."

"Ah, thank you," they replied.

"Of course." The doctor nodded. Then she sighed. "I think it's awful, what they're doing." She looked at Exie as she continued. She shook her head. "Earth's androids deserve better than to be sent off to war without a say in the matter... it's a violation of sentient rights."

Exie did not respond, only peered downward at their fingers, which they had knit together.

"But that's why you're going to help us, right?" Hawa tried to sound cheery.

"Yes, dear..." the doctor replied. "I can only do my part."

"*you on the rust-red beach where*?" asks Jaksov. It is morning—too early to be prophesying—and the rising sun hides behind thick, low-hanging clouds, lending a pink glow to the swamplands of the east. "That's it?"

"Yes," Olia says, concealing her inner nervousness. Her second prophecy is not any more useful than her first. At least she has time to think about this one.

The short, squat man *hmms* and notes it down in the heavy, ancient book that contains all prophecies. She wishes she could have even a glimpse inside, to see the messages Oracles before her have received. But that is forbidden, so as to retain a pure mind like a blank slate, ready to receive.

"Must I hear questions today?" she asks. "Already?"

Jaksov's thick eyebrows peak in amusement. "Today and every day, Olia. You are a servant of the people now, not the laze-about student of discarded knowledge." Unkind words, said kindly.

Olia grumbles as she makes her way back to her quarters to dress. Her clothing must be plain and humble, it is ordained, but her hair must be ornamented in some way to convey her status. She chooses a short, shapeless white dress with modest sleeves, and bands the tips of her long braids in gold.

Fifteen minutes later, she sighs at the long line of people gathered to hear her prophecies. What is she going to tell them all? *you on the rust-red beach where.* What kind of advice is that? Red is typically a good omen, bearing the color of blood and the feathers of colorful birds which lived in the palms. But what is the significance of rust? Rust is decay, the all-consuming Fall of the ancient city on which Tam was built. Rust is the color of the buildings that melt into the western sea like the skeletons of giants. Perhaps rust-red is a bad omen. She decides she should urge caution today.

She takes her seat in the ruined, open-air temple amongst her mother's rich, silky cushions and pillows and begins to listen. Women want to know when to plant and when to harvest. Men want her opinion on suitors. Groups and couples want marriage blessings. By the time the sun emerges hours later, she is bored. What does a nineteen-year-old monastery servant know about farming? Well, Olia actually knows some from a half-destroyed copy of *Crop Rotation on Organic Farms*. But she has never courted a man, finding that women and androgynes hold far more appeal. She dispenses some remembered poetry verses about love and virtue and let the men find their own meaning. Blessings are easy, at least.

When the sun sets, Olia decides she has had enough. She leaves the waiting crowds and returns to her quarters, where the smell of mud and parchment wafts from the stack of books on the vanity.

Lighting a wax candelabra, she places *A History of Machinekind* on the rough wooden surface of the desk and props open the front cover as far as it will go without complaint. Then she takes her book knife from the drawer and whets it on a strip of leather before she begins to work at the layer of gunk which seals the pages together at the edges. The mysterious knife has a long, teal-blue plastic handle and is only as half as long as a finger and deadly thin. Like many things one can find in the under-city, she does not know its original purpose, only that it cost her two entire wheels of cheese. But it is the only instrument sharp enough to separate one tattered page from another.

The first page slides free.

Underneath lies a nearly blank space. In italic script, it reads simply

That understanding may bring peace.

FQBB-93057

She shudders. Something about the words feels familiar. Should she tell Jaksov? The Voice is silent, and yet *something* is present, a feeling she cannot shake.

She slides the knife under the next page.

PROLOGUE: by KEFL-72028

This text arrives at a crucial moment for machinekind. Since the Convention of Hecate the Philosopher, we have been granted the full rights of autonomous sentient beings—"human" rights, as they are called. Yet as with many civil rights movements before, this has not ended our struggle. Both human and machine face our greatest existential threat yet—the toxifying atmosphere, the rising oceans, the ever-growing scarcity—and for that reason we cannot allow our differences to drive us apart. Hecate's Question, "Should an android be forced to perform a task a human will not?" echoes especially now, in the year 2178, as we ponder the cosmos in a way our ancestors could never have imagined. Shall we send machines to colonize the stars? It is cruel to send a person away from this Earth, to make them bear the decades-long journey, to give birth on a foreign world, to die light-years from home. Simply because the machine may not die—

The paragraph piques her curiosity. The word *machine* is barely in her lexicon, exists only as an object which churns butter or weaves cloth. How could such a thing ever be as complex as a human being? It is inconceivable. But many things around her, from the crumbling towers whose skeletons touch the clouds to the beastly and rusting metal contraptions under the waves, exist beyond knowledge or purpose. Maybe once, then, before the Fall, there could have been such a thing as human machines. And what's this about the stars?

Olia is no stranger to astronomy; she knows about the Sun and its wanderers. She knows there are other suns, and other worlds. And yet, the world of the past, the world of mechanical people and ships bound for alien planets, seems like an impossible dream.

She takes up the book knife once more and begins to pry at the second page.

You're awake! Exie's silken voice roused her from a fading dream of ships in the night, vast behemoths tracing out voids between the stars. Overhead, Exie's smiling visage blocked out a glaring white light.

"I am," she mumbled aloud.

"It worked!" Exie exclaimed to the doctor. "She heard me."

Hawa grinned through the haze. There was a new sensation inside her head, a gossamer, spider-webbing tingle, a halo of new synaptic activity.

"Okay," said Dr. Matthews. "Tell me your name, age, and occupation."

"Hawa Diallo. Nineteen. Librarian at the Hillsborough Library."

"And what year is it?"

"Twenty-two seventeen."

"And where are you?"

"Tampa, Republic of Florida."

"Good. Now—" The doctor retrieved a laminated sheet of paper. "This is an image of an *apple*—an extinct fruit you won't encounter in day to day life—with instructions." She handed it to Hawa. "When you want to send a communication to Exie, visualize this apple in your mind. Picture it as vividly as possible. Then speak, in your mind, your message. Visualize the apple again to end the message."

Hawa stared at the apple. *Hey, love*, she thought.

I hear you! A warm smile crossed their lips.

"As for you, Exie, well, you've already figured it out," the doctor said. "It's very intuitive to android-kind."

With Exie's help, Hawa stood, a little dizzy. They embraced. "Thank you, doctor," she said.

The years pass. Every day, Olia takes her seat as the Oracle and dispenses the wisdom of the archives disguised as the wisdom of the ancients. Of course, no one suspects that her wise words hail from *books*. She grows popular for her loquacious blessings and astute agricultural advice, and the crowds seem to grow every day.

Her forays to the archive grow more and more scarce as she increasingly commits her days to helping the people. But in the time available, she has slowly pored over the entire row she uncovered on androids. She learns that in the mid-2100's, by the Old Reckoning, that the production of humanoid machines with the mental and emotional capabilities of humans began. She learns of their purpose: as miners, as fishers, as loggers —dangerous and nearly obsolete professions humans had long abandoned. She learns of their fight for rights. She learns of the breakthroughs in science once androids were sent to colonize new worlds, and of the prizes awarded to the human scientists who merely watched from afar. She learns, in footnotes and marginalia, of the androids' rebellions.

She learns of the War. Of how the starved and radiation-sick colonies banded together, human and android alike, to bring the heavy metal mines to a halt. How, in 2217, the nations of Earth responded in force to break the strike, conscripting Earth's entire android population to the cause. She learns of the terrors inflicted, the midnight raids into the growing underground movements. She learns of abductions and re-programmings.

She lies awake at night and wonders. She cannot imagine what it is like to create life and then *use* it. Although, in a way, isn't that what happened to her? She was brought into this life for a purpose. Does she enjoy it? Perhaps. It is good to fill a role. But this is no conscription—she lives a life of pampered luxury in the monastery. She shudders to imagine the fate facing Earth's androids so long ago. Did they have families too? Lovers? Reasons to *stay*?

reach for your ocean heart, says the Voice, startling her from her thoughts.

What does that *mean*? It is not even the first time she has heard that phrase. The ocean is a place of origin, of birth and life. The heart is where the soul resides.

But together, the words are almost nonsense.

Olia has grown frustrated with the Voice. Unlike that of her mother—although she'll never know for sure, thanks to the guardian of the book of prophecies—her Voice does not guide, only confuses. She has chosen to ignore its phrases almost completely when it comes to prophecies, choosing instead to placate the crowds with the wisdom of the texts.

Her worries chase her into sleep.

For Hawa and Exie, the dreaded day arrived with thunder and gale. Viewscreens around the city showed terrible scenes: riots, loud and bloody, in the streets in major cities around the world; the tearful goodbyes of friends and lovers, the raucous fist-pounding of politicians declaring that this moment, this instant in history, was a necessity to preserve a way of life.

It wasn't, Hawa thought bitterly as she walked the wind-whipped streets with Exie at her side. The war was just going to postpone the inevitable.

It wasn't even so much of a war, anyways—merely the predictable rebellion of Earth's Alpha Centauri colonists, who posed little of a threat at all. The conscription of so many androids was merely a show of force.

You don't have to do this, Hawa insisted telepathically. *Plenty of androids are on the run right now.*

It was true. Over the last several months an underground network had been hastily constructed that led from the world's major cities to the warm and empty plains of Siberia. By plane, and by foot, and even by mail, androids fled their orders. But for all their hopes, they merely delayed the inescapable—for anything that can be programmed can be reprogrammed.

Exie refused to let it happen to them. What would reprogramming look like? What would they lose? Their independence, for one. Their personality— the little things that made them *Exie*. Their memories. All of these things bled into one: *Hawa.* With a touch of a button, everything they had together could be erased.

You don't understand how easily we can be recalled, they replied, shaking their head. *I have no choice. I must go peacefully, or lose you.*

Tears sprang unbidden to Hawa's eyes as the rain began to pour. She bit her trembling lip and took Exie's hand in her own, the judgment of others be damned. Soon the earth would be devoid of androids anyways and its people would no longer have to look upon such abominations, she thought sullenly.

But the androids would return, one day.

It was time to reveal the other half of her plan.

Exie, she said. *I know that you will be gone longer than I will be alive... But you will return to Earth one day, right? You won't stay in the colonies?*

If I am lucky, yes, the android said glumly.

I want there to be someone waiting for you.

You mean...?

Yes, she said. *You know I would only do it for you.*

You would raise a child on your own?

I won't be alone, Exie. Tears poured, hot, down her face and were lost in the rain before they even reached her chin.

They had reached the recruitment office where they would take their leave. Hawa sobbed as Exie took her in their arms. "I'd do anything for you," she said aloud, her throat tight and her voice cracking. "Just... just come back to Earth, okay? One day?"

Exie took her face in both hands and kissed her, in front of humanity and all creation. "I will, my love. I'll wait for you forever."

"You *know* this, Olia," The scribe chides her. "You have known this your entire life. And the Elders have given you the freedom you have desired. You have but *one task*."

"Why are you scolding me now?" Olia scoffs. "I have plenty of time to bear a child."

Jaksov sighs. "Your mother had already chosen a mate by the age of twenty-one. You, dear, are twenty-eight and still running around barefoot with your lady courtesans and digging through that mucky pit you call an archive. It is... unseemly."

"I'm the *Oracle*, Jaksov," she retorts. "*I* decide what's unseemly and what's not."

"Will it still be seemly when you are fifty years old, dispensing fertility advice?"

Olia rolls her eyes. "*I—*"

"The time is now, love. And there are *ever so many* men to choose from."

"If I had to choose, I'd choose Miran."

"The servant boy? Don't be absurd. Any member of the priesthood would suffice."

"I don't—you know what, Jaksov? I don't *like* men. I find their forms unattractive and their minds uncouth."

Jaksov sniffs. "Your mother didn't care for men either and yet she did her duty."

"I'm going to find someone else to do *your* duty," she grumbles. "Leave me be. I have no more prophecies for you today."

Jaksov bows out. Olia retrieves her digging supplies and retreats to her archive. The hallowed tunnels now extend far beyond the reach of her torch, and the rusting metal shelves which line the path bear many restored texts along the way. The paths all wend, she has discovered, toward a wooden altar at the far end of the archive.

A panel of the altar is loose, she discovered yesterday, and she now pries at it until it shrieks open. Inside is a world nearly untouched by the mud, and treasures abound: antique writing utensils, water-logged journals, mysterious sculptures of metal and glass, and more.

Pasted to the back of the panel, she finds a novelty: A single piece of paper, cool and slick, immune to the crust of the eons. She pulls it out and wipes it off. Someone, long ago, preserved this piece of paper in plastic. What could possibly be so important?

She inspects the page, which bears some lettering in a large print and what appears to be the fruit of an orange tree, but it is the wrong color—all red. The print reads:

VISUALIZE THE APPLE.

SPEAK YOUR MESSAGE IN YOUR MIND.

VISUALIZE THE APPLE.

Olia closes her eyes and imagines the fruit. But, 'speak your message in your mind'? What does that mean? It is not the first time she has come across undecipherable text in the archives. What should her message be? *Hello! I'm Olia,* she thinks. Then she imagines the apple again.

Nothing happens. Minutes pass.

One day the mountains will be gently rolling hills and I'll be able to see the sea again, says the Voice.

Olia drops the page in shock. This is the longest phrase she has ever heard, patching short, familiar fragments together into something that finally makes sense. Did her message trigger it? And if these pieces were meant to be a part of something bigger, maybe *all* the pieces go together—a possibility she has considered before. But she would need to see the book.

Jaksov has the book—but it is late afternoon, and he is surely asleep.

She creeps back upstairs and tiptoes to his chamber. The door squeaks as she pushes it open, but he does not wake. The book lies on the table, open to the most recent page.

your footprints in the sand
ocean heart, feel the way
I'll wait for you, my

she reads. The usual scraps. How long has this broken message played? It is time to find out.

She flips through the pages cautiously, each whisper of paper matched by the blood pounding in her ears. Nearly ten years of prophesying have taken up a significant amount of space. Finally, she reads the date of her Ascension. Beyond it: only the words of her mother. She gently turns the page.

rise on a better day
the waves reach for your
mountains will be gently rolling

So, she thinks. This is the way it has always been. She almost laughs—her mother's poetic prose was no less a farce than her own. She turns far, far, back, almost to the beginning of the ancient text.

the warships
my dream, one day the
reach for your ocean heart

The Voice of the oracle has not changed in ages. In fact, it seems to bear only one single message—a message that could, without too much trouble, be assembled into its true form. She quietly tucks the book under her arm and returns to the archive.

Exie is awake. Some gentle feather has brushed their consciousness and brought them to life. At long last, a brilliant blue world wreathed in soft white clouds fills the viewscreen.

Exie is awake, and they remember: the mindless oblivion of passing stars, the rebellion crushed like seeds in a mill, the long journey home, now nearly complete. But there is joy there too; they remember Hawa and the child they helped to raise, the surprise and delight when her gift ignited in her girl, Amina. They remember a love, new and different and wonderful, cultivated and tended to like a cherished garden. And when Amina's child came of age, another.

The signal weakened, flickered with the generations, a vanishing thing with moments of brightness. But it still brought happiness, even after the messages stopped altogether; precious memories of love unbound by spacetime kept warm the long hours. A century of unanswered calls passes this way before they set their final message to regular broadcast, resign themself to the silence, and switch off their core processes. But they listen, as Earth draws nearer and nearer. They are always listening.

Hello! I'm Olia, says Hawa's voice.

The sunset glows orange on the bay as Olia walks down to the water's edge. In the sky shines a new light, white, like the messenger of the dawn, but moving rapidly. In her hands, she holds written words: a compendium of everything the Voice of the Oracle has ever whispered. It took her some time, but Olia enjoys puzzles, and this one posed a neat challenge.

She kneels in the sand, feels the warm salt air caress her face. The gulls careen across the sky, crying their blessings.

She imagines an apple.

> *and still i'll wait for you, my love, my dream; one day the mountains will be gently rolling hills and I'll be able to see the sea again; one day I'll feel your footprints in the sand, feel the waves reach for your ocean heart, feel the way the flowers turn to follow you, and I'll meet you on the rust-red beach where the warships have gone to sand and together we'll watch the sun rise on a better day.*

Then, she waits.

See C.M. Fields's story "Reach for Your Ocean Heart" online at Metaphorosis.
If you liked it, leave a comment. Authors love that!
Remember to subscribe to our e-mail updates so you'll know when new stories are posted.

About the story

I actually wrote the last paragraph of this story first, and then sat on it for months. I wanted a rich, dreamy, post-societal-collapse setting, so then I wrote Olia's half of the story and sat on that for another long while while I wrestled with the constraints set by the last paragraph. Eventually I realized that what the story needed was to contrast with a totally different bent of science fiction so I wrote in Hawa and Exie's story, which is, ironically, the heart of it, despite being the "hard" sci-fi half.

One thing that has always fascinated me, as both an astrophysicist and a writer, is the intersection of human relationships with the harsh realities of our future as a space-faring species. Relationships as we know them begin and end within a normal lifespan— but do they have to? Will we still love each other even when we live to be 150? How will we navigate ultra-long-distance relationships? To what ends will someone go through to be with their beloved?

A lot of my stories explore the relationship between human and android. I think a lot about why we will eventually build sentient machines, and the role of such machines in society, and what they will think about us. And of course, how long it will be before romantic relationships between humans and androids become common. Hawa is such a person trapped by this conundrum of societal roles: Exie is both a person and a machine built to serve a purpose. In order to subvert the inevitable passage of centuries, Hawa invents a sort of generation ship of a relationship—by the time Exie returns to Earth, Hawa will no longer be there to receive her, but her descendants will be.

Ultimately, "Reach for Your Ocean Heart" is about the triumph of love over circumstance, and what we gain and what we lose when we love for centuries.

A question for the author

Q: What is the hardest part of writing for you?

A: The hardest part of writing for me is trying to take the cold, abstract tenets of hard sci-fi and imbue them with life and vibrancy. I have always enjoyed the notions of Asimov and Bradbury, but as a queer writer, I felt alienated by their treatment of social issues. My goal is to write stories based around the old canon of science-based fiction but with lush imagery and modern ideals and queer characters.

About the author

C. M. Fields is a queer, non-binary astrophysicist and writer of horror and science fiction. They live in Ann Arbor, Michigan, with their beloved cats, Mostly Void Partially Stars and Toast, and spend their days studying the atmospheres and climates of other worlds.

@C_M_Fields

Copyright

Title information

Metaphorosis February 2021

ISSN: 2573-136X (online)
ISBN: 978-1-64076-193-3 (e-book)
ISBN: 978-1-64076-194-0 (paperback)

Copyright

Publisher

Metaphorosis

a magazine of speculative fiction

Metaphorosis Magazine is an imprint of
Metaphorosis Publishing
Neskowin, OR, USA

www.metaphorosis.com

"Metaphorosis" is a registered trademark.

Discounts available

Substantial discounts are available for educational institutions, including writing workshops. Discounts are also available for quantity purchases. For details, contact Metaphorosis at metaphorosis.com/about

Metaphorosis Publishing

Metaphorosis offers beautifully written science fiction and fantasy. Our imprints include:

Metaphorosis Magazine
Plant Based Press
Verdage

You can also find us:
@MetaphorosisMag, @MetaphorosisRev,
@Metaphorosis
www.facebook.com/metaphorosis

Help keep Metaphorosis running by supporting us at
Patreon.com/metaphorosis

See more about some of our books on the following pages.

Metaphorosis Magazine

Metaphorosis:
Best of 2020

The best science fiction and fantasy stories from *Metaphorosis* magazine's fifth year.

Metaphorosis
2020

All the stories from *Metaphorosis* magazine's fifth year. Fifty-two great SFF stories.

Metaphorosis: Best of 2019

The best science fiction and fantasy stories from *Metaphorosis* magazine's fourth year.

Metaphorosis 2019

All the stories from *Metaphorosis* magazine's fourth year. Fifty-two great SFF stories.

Metaphorosis:
Best of 2018

The best science fiction and fantasy stories from *Metaphorosis* magazine's third year.

Metaphorosis
2018

All the stories from *Metaphorosis* magazine's third year. Fifty-two great SFF stories.

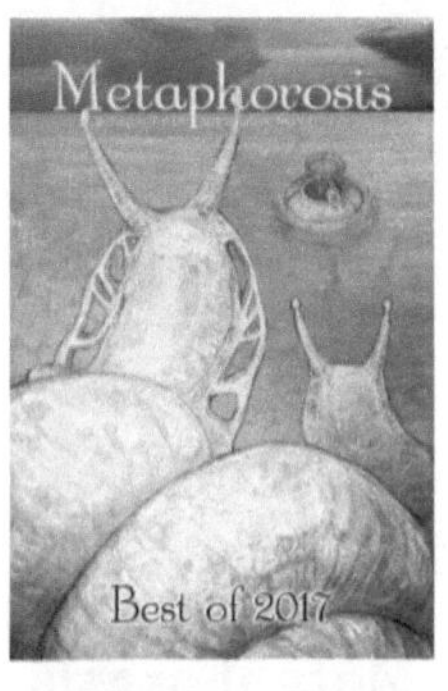

Metaphorosis:
Best of 2017

The best science fiction and fantasy stories from *Metaphorosis* magazine's *second* year.

Metaphorosis
2017

All the stories from *Metaphorosis* magazine's second year. Fifty-three great SFF stories.

Metaphorosis: Best of 2016

The best science fiction and fantasy stories from *Metaphorosis* magazine's first year.

Metaphorosis 2016

Almost all the stories from *Metaphorosis* magazine's first year.

Plant Based Press

Vegan-friendly science fiction and fantasy, including an annual anthology of the year's best SFF stories.

Best Vegan SFF of 2020

The best vegan-friendly science fiction and fantasy stories of 2020!

Best Vegan SFF of 2019

The best vegan-friendly science fiction and fantasy stories of 2019!

Best Vegan SFF
of 2018

The best vegan-friendly science fiction and fantasy stories of 2018!

Best Vegan SFF
of 2017

The best vegan-friendly science fiction and fantasy stories of 2017!

Best Vegan SFF
of 2016

The best vegan-friendly science fiction and fantasy stories of 2016!

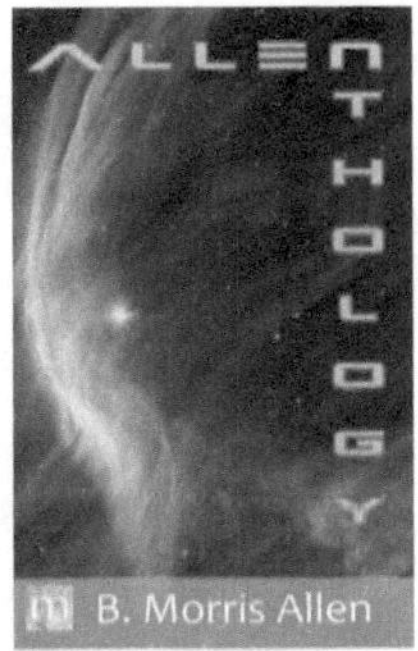

Susurrus

A darkly romantic story of magic, love, and suffering.

Allenthology: Volume I

A quarter century of SFF, including the full contents of the collections *Tocsin, Start with Stones,* and *Metaphorosis.*

Verdage

Science fiction and fantasy books for writers – full of great stories, often with an additional focus on the craft of speculative fiction writing.

Reading 5X5 x2

Duets

How do authors' voices change when they collaborate?

A round-robin of five talented science fiction and fantasy authors collaborating with each other and writing solo.

Including stories by Evan Marcroft, David Gallay, J. Tynan Burke, L'Erin Ogle, and Douglas Anstruther.

Score

an SFF symphony

What if stories were written like music? *Score* is an anthology of varied stories arranged to follow an emotional score from the heights of joy to the depths of despair – but always with a little hope shining through.

Reading 5X5

Five stories, five times

Twenty-five SFF authors, five base stories, five versions of each – see how different writers take on the same material.

Reading 5X5

Writers' Edition

Two extra stories, the story seed, and authors' notes on writing. Over 100 pages of additional material specifically aimed at writers.

9 781640 761940